Copyright © 2024 by Niamh Davies

All rights reserved. No part of this publication may be reproduced, distributed, or transmitted in any form or by any means, including photocopying, recording, or other electronic or mechanical methods, without the prior written permission of the publisher, except in the case of brief quotations embodied in critical reviews and certain other non-commercial uses permitted by copyright law.

Published by Niamh Davies

ISBN: 9798883643872

Printed in the United Kingdom

Printed by Kindle Direct Publishing

For permissions requests, please contact: nquinxly@gmail.com

Some language and descriptions may be upsetting if you are sensitive to blood, gore, or violence. Read at your discretion.

The Maple Murders
Written by Niamh Davies

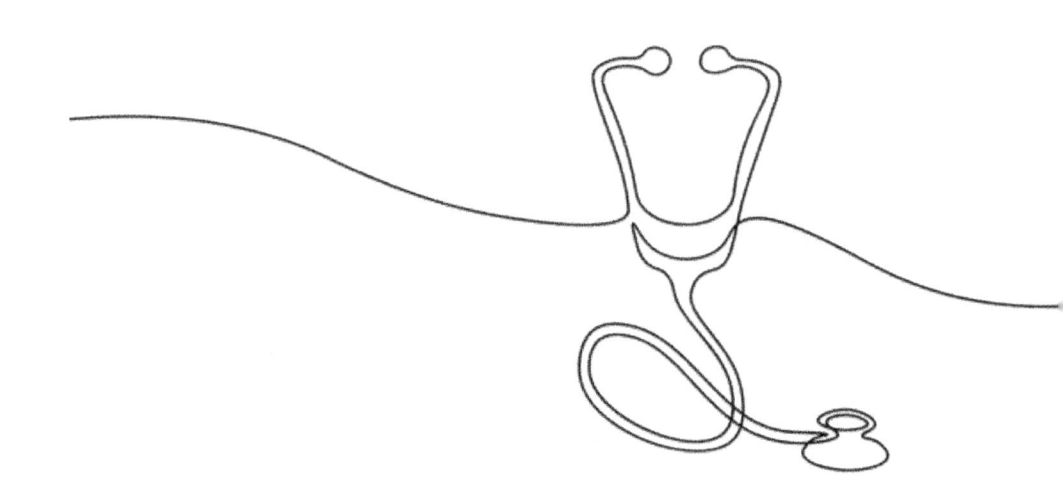

Author's note

Please be advised that this novel contains explicit language and scenes that may be disturbing to some readers. Furthermore, I apologize for any inconsistencies or lack of realism; my research was limited to Google. Additionally, I lack experience in graphic design and lack the funds to hire a professional, so I apologize for the awful quality of the cover. I also have no idea what I'm doing.

Thank you for your understanding.

Anyways, enjoy! <3

*"Bad things happen to the people you love,
and you'll find yourself praying to the heaven above.
But honestly, I've never had much sympathy,
'Cause those bad things, I always saw them coming for me."*
--Bad things, Cults

Chapter 1
A flouted promise.

Friday, 25th of November 2022.

The trees rustled with a static sound, battling against the rough wind that pushed through their branches. Raindrops raced down the window as a result of the harsh stormy weather outside. Inside, the incessant beeping of Ellie's heart monitor punctuated the air with each heartbeat. It was almost like a countdown, but nobody knows when that countdown will end, or if there even was an ending. Perhaps this steady beep would persist as long as Ash lived, a haunting reminder of Ellie's struggles. Or maybe the beeping will come to an end. For better, or for worse.

It was two o'clock in the afternoon. Ash was sitting on the baby-blue leather chair, positioned across from her daughter Ellie's bed. Dark, heavy bags swelled under her eyes, and her black knotted hair was a testament to the long nights she spent at the hospital. She wore her usual oversized black and grey stripy jumper, paired with dark ripped jeans and worn-out converse.

The exhausted look on her face was enough evidence to tell that she hasn't rested in days, but there is no such thing as 'rest' when your 6-year-old daughter is dying on a hospital bed. There's no break from the constant anxiety which flows through your veins, as if it's become a part of your blood. There's no break from the overwhelming thought of your own daughter's grave. But here Ellie was, lying peacefully in her bed like there's not a problem in the world.

Ash was startled by the knock on the door. A tall, young woman who appeared to be no older than 30, entered the room. "Good afternoon, Ash," The woman said with a gentle smile. It was Ellie's doctor, Doctor Nia Quinn. She was wearing a long polyester lab coat, a dark blue scrub shirt, black trousers, and a high-quality pair of shoes - so high-quality, one would think they were brand new. Her long, black hair was tucked behind her black glasses, and a facemask hung from her ear. "How's Ellie holding up?" She asked.

Ash gave a blank, tired stare. "She hasn't moved in days."

"Fortunately, her condition is improving." Quinn replied. "The X-rays confirm that the fluid is slowly disappearing, and she's responding well to the digoxin."

They remained silent for a moment before Quinn sighed and looked at Ash. "You've been sitting in this room for days, why don't you get a snack from the café?"

"No." Ash snapped. "I'm not hungry." The growl coming from her stomach says otherwise.

"Come on, Ash." Quinn explained. "You know it's important to look after yourself." Quinn gave Ash a reassuring smile. "Ellie will be completely fine in the short time that you're gone. I *promise*."

After another short moment of silence, Ash stood up and approached Ellie's bed. She bent over and kissed the child's forehead lightly. "Mommy will be back soon, okay? I love you." Ash then turned around and left the room.

Ash slowly made her way down the dim hallway and arrived at the café soon afterward. "A coffee, please." She asked the man working behind the counter. As she waited for her coffee, her nose was filled with the scents of freshly brewed coffee mixing with the chlorine coming from the cleaner's mop bucket. Opposite her stood a few wooden tables and chairs. A large teal-blue painted wall and an old coffee stain on the floor were also visible, and… A woman.

"Hey, Ash!" She heard a familiar voice shout from somewhere in the dim hallway. It was one of Ash's co-workers, Emma. Despite the fact that Ash wouldn't consider her a *'friend'* – in fact, not anyone for that matter – she remained courteous. Since her daughter's diagnosis, Ash had always remained closed off, choosing to prioritize Ellie above all others. A few years ago, however, Ash had been a completely different woman with a husband, friends, and a sense of contentment. Unfortunately, Ash's life had changed swiftly, but no one knew why.

Emma was wearing her typical light blue scrubs, as well as her red stethoscope hanging around her neck, and her light brown hair tied up in a ponytail. "A coffee for me too, please!" Emma said as she approached the counter.

The two seated themselves beside the railings, enjoying the view of the main reception from above.

"So, how have you been?" Emma asked in her typical friendly voice. "Feels like we haven't spoken in weeks!"

Emma appeared to seem eager to start a conversation with Ash.

Ash responded quickly, trying to keep her voice calm and collected. "Anxious about Ellie," she said, though "anxiety" did not even compare to the magnitude of emotions she was currently feeling. The passage of time was her enemy, for every minute seemed like an unbearable eternity of soul-crushing anguish and torment.

Every small detail Ash observed seemed to trigger memories of her daughter, whether she wanted them to or not. The smell of coffee took her back to busy school mornings with Ellie, where they'd rush to leave the house on time. The waiting area reminded her of when Ellie and her ex-husband would sit and wait for her to finish her shift. Even the soft hum of the air conditioning in the background made her think of the times when she'd come home from work and Ellie would be asleep on the couch, snoring softly.

But what caused her the most pain and heartache was the agonizing feeling of guilt that washed over her every time she spotted parents with their children, happy and unburdened by the worries of a sick child. It was like being stabbed in the stomach with a sharp sword; a constant, painful reminder of how she had failed to keep Ellie safe, how she failed as a parent. The sight made Ash seethe with anger, and she felt an uncontrollable urge to see those parents and their children perish. That way, there would be no other parents for her to compare herself to, and her pain and suffering would finally feel justified.

Ash stared directly into her coffee with an impassive expression, ignoring any opportunity to engage in small talk. Emma looked up alarmed. "Oh, that's right! I've completely forgotten. How is Ellie doing?"

Ash remained silent for a moment before responding, "She hasn't moved in days."

Emma tried to be reassuring, though reassurance isn't her strongpoint. "Doctor Quinn is one of this hospital's most trusted doctors. She will fix Ellie up in no time."

Ash still appeared distant, ignoring Emma's attempt at comfort. She looked down at her coffee, not wanting to remember her daughter. "She used to sing songs… play with her toys, and constantly bicker about that game she loves." Ash said. "Now, I would do *anything* to hear her talk again."

An awkward silence fell over them as they both stared intently at their coffees. The silence was soon broken by the sound of an announcement on the income speaker.

9

"Code blue in room 202," the voice over the speakers said.

It was in that moment that Ash's life changed forever. Her heart dropped as she froze in a state of dread. The colour drained from her face as her legs turned to jelly. Regret filled her body as the worst-case scenario had come true. Within seconds, Ash ran up from her seat, abandoning her coffee and her colleague as she sprinted to her daughter's room. It felt as though she was drowning in her own dread, or even burning alive in her own regret.

Ash slammed through the door, where she saw Doctor Quinn performing chest compressions on Ellie, surrounded by countless other recognizable faces - all dressed in hospital uniform. Ash rushed over to the chaos happening in front of them, pushing the staff out of the way. "ELLIE!" She screamed as tears poured down her face.

"Emma, prepare the AED." Doctor Quinn shouted over the overwhelming sound of alarms and flat-line beeps coming from the heart monitor. It was like a soul-crushing nightmare that Ash couldn't awaken from. Beside Ash stood Doctor Daniel Graham, another one of Ash's co-workers.

"What are you doing?!" Ash exclaimed to Graham in a panic, before pushing him into the crowd of staff. "Don't just stand there, do something!"

Seconds turned to minutes as Ash anxiously waited for Ellie's heart to beat. The defibrillator shocked Ellie multiple times, but the alarms continued to scream in Ash's ears.

'Please hold on, Ellie… Hold on baby girl, I need you…' Ash begged to herself silently as she helplessly watched the staff struggle to keep Ellie

alive, but when Emma approached her and dragged her out of the room, Ash realized it was too late.

"Where are you taking me?! What's going on?!" Ash cried in panic, though the answer was clear to see.

Emma's tone was heavy as she delivered the devastating news. "I'm so sorry Ash, but Ellie didn't make it."

Her pupils contracted drastically, and her voice beginning to tremble. The bitter taste of bile lingered at the back of her throat, weighting her entire being as she struggled to come to terms with the terrible news.

"W... What...?"

"Ellie has passed away, November 25th, 2022. Two twenty-one PM."

And with the passing of Ellie, Ash's world turned as cold and dark as a winter moonless night. She had lost everyone and everything to the cruel hands of fate, and to her it felt as though her life was no longer her own. Every day that passed was nothing more than another reminder of the life she had lived, the life she had lost, and the life that would never again be. She was no longer a mother, a daughter, or even a human being - she was a shell, a shadow, and an empty vessel awaiting the sweet release of death.

Chapter 2
Painted in crimson.

Sunday, January 8th, 2023.

It had been a little over a month since Ellie's passing. Ash was laying on the disreputable couch in her living room, surrounded by empty coke cans and dirty plates scattered around the room. On the wooden coffee table opposite her sat countless bottles of whiskey, vodka, ash trays and used cigarettes, along with a scruffy notebook, pen and other random accessories. The muffled sound of the TV in the background did little to muffle the silence, but it helped to make time pass quicker.

Ash looked as though she hasn't washed her hair in months. The bags under her eyes had grown ten times heavier and darker.

There was a knock at the door, but Ash wasn't startled this time. She didn't even notice it until someone knocked harder on the window. When she finally realized that someone was there, she sighed and slowly stood up, her head pounding in her skull as the world around her spun. This was probably the first time she had gotten up all day - even though it was already 2 PM.

Ash took a peep through the door's peephole, where she spotted Quinn standing opposite the door. Of all the people in the world, why did it have to be *her*? Despite her hatred, she opened the door.

"Whatcha' want...?" she asked with clear annoyance in her tone.

Quinn's smile wavered when Ash spoke; it was like Ash completely forgot how to socialize after blocking everyone out for so long. Quinn noticed the dirty dressing gown that Ash wore, along with the rough appearance on her face. The strong smell of alcohol and cigarettes emanating from her only added to the picture of neglect and isolation.

"Good afternoon." Quinn spoke in an awkward manner. "I know it's odd timing, but no one has heard from you in weeks… I wanted to check in and make sure things were alright."

"Yeah," Ash answered quickly before attempting to shut the door, but before it could shut, Quinn reached out and stopped the door in its tracks.

"Hold on," Quinn said. "I was wondering if I could step inside and have a quick chat?"

"No," Ash responded firmly.

"Okay," Quinn said. "How about a walk instead?"

Ash paused at the thought. After Ellie's passing, Ash had been thinking of ways to get her revenge on Quinn for failing to save her daughter. The mere thought of Quinn going about her life with impunity after the heartbreaking incident had kept Ash awake during long, sleepless nights. However, the opportunity to get revenge presented itself perfectly.

"Fine," Ash replied, trying to conceal the anger and hatred she held for the woman standing opposite her. She stepped away from the door and said, "I'll go and get ready." This gave Ash a chance to get her emotions in check and prepare herself to put on a mask, which would hide her true feelings towards Quinn.

As Ash quickly shut the door, she felt a small spark of excitement for the first time since Ellie's diagnosis. After brushing her hair and changing out of her pyjamas, she began to search the house for a tool, feeling that this opportunity for revenge would be a perfect way to channel her grief and anger. With a spring in her step, Ash returned to the kitchen and spotted a hammer on the counter. She had used it a few months ago when attempting to repair the kitchen counter, but now it could be used for a much more gruesome job.

"Ready," she shouted to Quinn after hiding the hammer in the bottom of her bag and stepping back outside.

"So…" Quinn began as they walked down the neighbourhood path. "How have you been?"

Ash answered with clear frustration. "Great. Absolutely great," she said bitterly, almost as bitter as the winter afternoon's breeze. Her tone indicated the exact opposite. Quinn looked away in embarrassment at Ash's response. She knew Ash was upset but didn't expect her to lash out at her.

Ash then continued, this time with a calmer tone. "I'm angry. I'm upset. I miss Ellie." This was the first time she had admitted aloud how much she still missed her daughter.

Quinn regarded Ash with a look of compassion. "I'm so sorry, I can't even imagine losing a child."

Ash glared back at her with a stony expression. "It's a good thing it isn't you then, isn't it?" She replied in a huff. With that, an awkward silence fell between them, and they continued walking past the neighbourhood play park in silence.

"Ash, I know that you're upset—," Quinn began, but was immediately cut off as a spark of rage flickered in Ash's eyes.

Ash's voice was suddenly loud and sharp, piercing through Quinn's ears. "You have no idea what I'm going through," Ash snapped. "After the miscarriage, the divorce…" Her voice was filled with emotion, as months' worth of bottled-up anger and sadness came pouring out. "Ellie was all I had left. And you took her from me…"

The fire in her eyes burned with the weight of all the burdens she had been carrying since the day of Ellie's passing. Quinn stepped back in fear as Ash erupted in rage. She had never seen Ash in such a state, and her attempt to calm her down was like pouring gasoline on a burning pyre.

"Look," Quinn said, trying again to reassure Ash. She wasn't finished yet, though; Ash quickly snapped back, "Now you're going to fucking pay for it."

Ash's blood began to boil as her emotions ran rampant. The winter's cold, sharp breeze blew past her face, but she was far beyond being calmed down by anything, even by the harsh weather. Her anger consumed her, fuelling her with uncontrollable rage.

In a single swift action, Ash snatched the hammer out of her bag and swung it against Quinn's head with a brutal, unanticipated force – a force so strong that no rational person could have imagined it. Before Quinn could even react, she flew to the ground in a single hit, but Ash didn't stop there. The feeling of revenge was too exciting, and so she continued to beat Quinn to death and beyond.

The warm, dark crimson of Quinn's blood erupted violently from her temple, staining Ash's clothes in a macabre display. At first, it surged quick and powerful, but with each passing moment, its flow slowed to a sluggish trickle from her wounds.

Murdering Quinn in broad daylight beside a busy hospital was a very risky move, but luck was on Ash's side. They were alone, and she acted quickly, leaving no chance for witnesses.

The adrenaline hit its peak, and Ash felt a chilling sense of satisfaction with each strike of the hammer. With bloodlust in her eyes, she stared at Quinn's brutalized form, the spattered droplets of blood tracing dark red paths down Ash's face and onto her clothes.

The sight before Ash was a brutal sight not meant for the faint of heart. Crimson streams painted most of Quinn's face, glistening in the muted sunlight as they trailed down her cheeks, mingling with her hair, and pooling in gruesome puddles on the floor below. Chunks of flesh, resembling macabre puzzle pieces, were displaced, while silvers of glass from her shattered glasses cut deep lines across her skin.

Beneath the thick layer of blood, the unforgiving aftermath revealed silvers of bone and shards of broken skull, a testament to the violence inflicted. Yet amidst this carnage, Quinn's body remained oddly untouched, save for the saturation of her clothes with the evidence of her ordeal.

Ash tried to catch her breath, but the adrenaline still running high in her veins made it difficult. Despite the horror of what she had just done, Ash felt a sense of pride in her accomplishment.

"*You motherfucker.*" She muttered under her breath.

For the first time in months, Ash felt a sensation that was entirely unfamiliar to her. It was a feeling so distant from anything she had experienced in years, that it left her utterly confused and disoriented. A weight that she had been carrying on her shoulders for far too long seemed to have disappeared in an instant, yet she felt an overwhelming sense of emptiness and nothingness. It was as if the constant guilt, regret, and hatred that had consumed her every waking moment had suddenly evaporated, and she was left with nothing but a sense of surreal calm.

Ash took a deep breath, breathing in the cool winter air and feeling it fill her lungs and clear her mind. It was as if the lump in her throat, which had been a constant companion for months, had finally vanished. She felt free, and she was able to finally breathe – finally live -- after so many months of being trapped in a cycle of self-loathing and despair.

"Chaotic shift!" Emma said as she exited the hospital's side entrance with Rosa. Rosa Sharma - or sometimes known as 'Rose', is one of the nicest people Emma knows; some might even say she is the nicest person in the entire hospital. Rosa wore dark blue scrubs, large thin glasses, and occasionally a white lab coat. Her dark caramel skin always had a sweet vanilla aroma, and her black hair was always wrapped in a bun.

"You said it!" Rosa concurred, smiling kindly. Her smile never failed to leave a warm sensation of butterflies in Emma's stomach. "I have some errands to run this afternoon, so I must be on my way," she replied. "See you later!"

And with that, Rosa waved goodbye and headed to her car to get on with the many tasks that awaited her this afternoon.

As Emma bid farewell with a wave, her gaze chanced upon something in the far-off distance.

"Huh?" she murmured; her attention snagged by the shadowy silhouette as she gazed at the shadowy figure. It felt as if a magnetic force of curiosity was pulling her closer, like something was left there for the purpose of being found.

Approaching cautiously, confusion soon gave way to stark horror as recognition dawned on her. A motionless figure laid still on the ground, its identity slowly crystallizing in Emma's mind. It took her a moment to realize her initial disbelief with the chilling reality: a person, lifeless and prone.

With each step forward, Emma's heart pounded in her chest, the frigid air catching in her shallow breaths. She desperately clung to the hope that it might be a fallen branch or sleeping animal, any explanation other than the unthinkable. Yet, as she drew nearer, the truth become inescapable, and a single, trembling question escaped her lips: "Quinn…?"

With the name barely a whisper, Emma's worst fears were confirmed. She approached the body with cautious steps, unable to tear her gaze away from the sight of the mangled and bloodied figure.

A primal scream of pain and anguish escaped from Emma's mouth as she realized the extent of the tragedy before her, a sound that echoed through the empty neighbourhood like a cry of terror. The scene was unbearable. Amidst the bloodied clothes and shattered glasses, the only evidence of Quinn's identity lay in ruins. Her disfigured face left a painful mark of trauma on Emma's mind. Greyish skin and the scent of fresh blood permeated the air, intensifying the horror.

Despite Emma's experience as a nurse, she had never encountered anything like this. This wasn't just a tragedy; it was a deliberate act of murder.

Collapsing onto her knees, then onto the unforgiving ground, Emma found herself immobilized by shock. Tears streamed down her face in torrents, her chest convulsing with each sob. Not only was she Quinn's nursing assistant, but the two were close friends for a few years, and their friendship ended with a tragic outcome.

"W-Who… Who did this to you…?" Emma sobbed. "How… Why… W-What happened?!"

The thought of never seeing Quinn again made her feel like she was being torn apart from the inside out. The pain in her heart was unbearable, and no amount of questioning would change the reality that Quinn was gone *forever*.

Despite the crushing weight of her sorrow, Emma knew she couldn't remain paralyzed by despair. With trembling resolve, she made a silent vow to carry on, no matter how hard it might be. Though the pain of loss would never leave her, Emma was determined to forge ahead, one agonizing step at a time.

Emma casted one last glance at Quinn before sprinting to the director's office, dread consuming her with every step. The image of Quinn's lifeless form continued to haunt her, each recollection triggering fresh tears and sobs.

In the corridor's eerie silence, Emma's footsteps echoed her inner turmoil. She hesitated for a moment, grappling with the weight of what she had just witnessed. With a heavy sigh, she turned away from the haunting scene, determined to face the challenging ordeal that awaited her in the director's office.

Chapter 3
Brutal Honesty

3:40 PM

The cold, winter air hung heavily with the sound of screeching tires and blaring sirens as police cars surrounded the crime scene beside the hospital. A crowd of curious bystanders had gathered, craning their necks to see over the yellow tape that cordoned off the area. The flashing blue and red lights of the police cars reflected off the glass and stone walls of the hospital, creating an eerie glow in the otherwise darkening evening. The air was tense and uncomfortable, punctuated by hushed whispers among the onlookers, who each carried the knowledge that someone had been murdered, but not who or why.

The uneasiness caused by death is not uncommon when working at a hospital, as some lives can be saved while others cannot. It's a simple factor of life that all medical professionals must come to terms with. *This* uneasy feeling was different, though. This was no ordinary death; it was a murder - the murder of one of the hospital's most respected doctor, that is.

"What were you doing when you discovered the murder?" The middle-aged police officer asked Emma while scribbling down notes on a clipboard.

"I had just finished my shift..." Emma explained, speaking through a veil of distress. "After waving goodbye to my friend Rosa, a figure in the distance caught my eye... When I got closer, I realized it was Quinn."

Yet another wave of tears filled her eyes as Emma continued to describe the gruesome scene. "Her face was unrecognizable," she said through her sobs. As the horrific images of Quinn's brutalized face filled her head, she couldn't help but break into yet another outburst of tears.

"And what happened after that?" The man inquired, as if trying to make sense of the disturbing events that took place. Emma went on to describe how she ran to the director's office in search of help. Soon after, the police officer finished his questionnaire and allowed Emma to leave.

"A murder?! I can't believe it!" exclaimed Doctor Joel Anderson as he observed the crime scene from behind the yellow tape. Anderson, a man in his late fifties with a short beard and short brown hair, a greyish lab coat, light teal shirt, and black trousers, was the hospital's director. He had over 30 years of experience and was known to be one of the most respected and knowledgeable doctors in the hospital. Despite his stern demeanour, his staff knew him to be one of the kindest and most light-hearted people they had the pleasure to work with.

As Anderson observed the crime scene from behind the yellow tape, the young woman, Kat Parker, who stood next to him, chimed in. "I know, right," she said, a cocky tone colouring her words.

Known for her short temper and annoying demeanour, Kat Parker was Anderson's assistant and had a reputation for being useless and making everyone's life hell. The most troublesome aspect of her, though, is the relationship she shared with Anderson, which is a "father-daughter" dynamic that makes it impossible to raise any complaints about her behaviour.

"I bet it was Emma!" Kat shouted, a delighted tone colouring her words. Unlike most in the hospital, Kat was more concerned with drama than feelings.

Joel looked at her with a stern yet kind expression, "Please don't point fingers without proof. We need evidence before throwing accusations around."

Kat rolled her eyes, "Emma found the body. That's all the evidence we need."

Joel sighed with slight irritation, "Go tell the department managers there's a meeting in my office in an hour."

With that, Kat left in a huff, like a dog dutifully following its master.

"Emma!" Joel called from across the scene, beckoning Emma to approach him. He made a "come here" motion with his hand, and she walked over, still sobbing from earlier. "I'm sorry you had to find out about Quinn this way," he said. "Are you alright?"

"Shocked... distraught to say the least," Emma said, wiping the tears from her eyes.

"I'm here for you if you need any extra support," Joel offered, before adding, "Just wanted to let you know that there's a meeting at my office in an hour. It's necessary that you come along as you discovered the body."

Emma nodded her head. "I'll go there now. I need a quiet place to process my emotions," she said before making her way to the office.

Emma made her way to the staff room -- a large, open space with a small brown couch, two teal chairs, a wooden coffee table with a TV opposite it, and a small, modern kitchen on the other side. At the far end of the room was another door, with a sign reading "Director's Office".

Emma seated herself on the brown couch and buried her head in her hands, seeking for a moment of silence. However, her peace was shaken by the Director's office door swinging open.

"Hello, Emma." Kat said as she exited the office into the staffroom, her face plastered with a sly expression that Emma ignored. After all, Kat's constant lectures had become part of everyday life, but they were the least of Emma's worries.

"Hi, Kat." Emma responded, her tone indifferent as she focused on other things.

"What brings you here? Are you planning to murder me next?" Kat said, her usual cocky tone making Emma roll her eyes. But the final sentence caught her attention.

"Excuse me?" Emma asked.

"I know what you did." Kat said, her expression suddenly becoming serious.

Despite Emma's annoyance, she couldn't deny that she was now intrigued. "Kat, please don't mess around; I'm begging you. Not now." she begged, making her way to the office door, hoping to catch a break from her annoying boss. Kat slammed the door aggressively as she gave Emma a deadly glare.

"Not so fast." She ordered. "The meeting hasn't started yet, and as Anderson's assistant, I cannot allow you to enter his office without his consent."

As if the day couldn't get any worse, Emma was now confronted with Kat, trying to ruin her day even more with her constant controlling blabber.

"In the meantime," Kat added, "I'm going to make you admit that you murdered Nia."

Emma felt her blood boiling as her patience was put to the ultimate test. She knew she had to keep her anger in check, but it was easier said than done. Kat was out for her blood, and she wasn't going to stop until she'd broken Emma.

Emma paused in astonishment; she simply couldn't believe what she was hearing. Just when she thought that Kat couldn't sink any lower, she does so with ease. She couldn't even bring herself to form words for a moment. "What did you say?" she finally muttered.

"You heard me," Kat sneered. "How could you do such a thing? Nia was such a kind, young, talented woman with so much potential. All the lives she could've saved, but instead a greedy monster came along to take her position and ended up taking her life."

Emma was almost speechless as flashbacks of discovering Quinn's lifeless body flooded her mind. Kat's taunting and lecturing pushed her past the breaking point, causing yet another flood of tears to run down her cheeks. "I-I didn't-" she started, but Kat cut her off with more sickening accusations.

"Come on, Emma. You were standing over her dead body," Kat said. Every word she spoke felt like a pinprick across her skin, making her want to disappear. Being wrongly blamed for something so horrible was almost as painful as discovering the corpse.

"She... She was one of my closest friends..." Emma muttered.

"You'll be in handcuffs before you know it! Sick and twisted people like you deserve to burn in h—" Kat's words were forced to stop as Emma's hand slapped across her face.

"What in the name of heaven is happening here?" Anderson demanded, speaking in a tone that suggested both shock and exasperation. Emma took a few timid steps in the opposite direction, feeling humiliated while Kat continued her absurd tirade.

"She confessed it!" Kat raved. "She's a murderer. You saw her attack me just now, didn't you? Do something. Call the--."

"In my office, NOW!" There was no mistaking the anger in Anderson's voice when he shouted his demand. A second man stood next to Anderson, wearing a similar outfit, consisting of a teal-coloured shirt, a dark grey tie, and an old greyish lab coat with navy trousers held up by a belt. The man had short, black hair and thin black glasses. His presence and attitude suggested that he was a person of significance.

Kat entered the office with determination in her stride, while Anderson turned to face Emma with a hint of anger in his voice.

"Correct me if I'm wrong," he said. "But did you just slap Kat?"

Emma looked up at him, her expression reflecting the anxiety she felt. "I-I'm sorry... I didn't kill Nia," she wept. "I swear on my life, I didn't."

Anderson took a deep breath as the man beside him watched attentively. "I know, Emma," he said quietly. "I knew from the moment you came to seek my help."

Emma wiped the tears from her face, sniffling and attempting to hold back her sobs. "Why did she blame me?"

Anderson placed a reassuring hand on Emma's shoulder, trying to comfort her as best he could. "Kat is very desperate to find Nia's murderer," he explained, "so desperate that she's blaming staff with little to no evidence." He then looked at the other man next to him and made an introduction. "This is Doctor Neil David," he said, "he's the chief pathologist. You two stay here, I'll sort out Kat."

With that, Anderson entered his office, leaving Emma and David behind.

3:50 PM

Ash being tucked up in her bed, be it at 5 in the afternoon or 11 in the morning, was nothing new. For many months now, her bed had been a place to ignore reality – a place of solitude, yet also a place of imprisonment.

It felt like heaven to be able to find refuge in her bed after the endless days of trauma and stress, but felt like hell to feel trapped and confined to this space that she felt she could never escape from. As if her body were being weighed down with bricks, becoming too heavy to move. Her motivation turned to dust in an instant, leaving her with a sense of hopelessness and powerlessness.

There was no reason for Ash to leave her bed. Not for her mail, not for the person knocking at the door, not even for herself. Whether she wanted to or not, this bittersweet space became her home and her prison. When she falls asleep, she is tormented by nightmares. Even after countless hours or days of trying to rest, she finds herself restless and awake. This poignant comfort becomes both torture and solace, pushing Ash to the brink of her existence and beyond.

Today was different, though. Ash felt comfortable in her bed, as her head lay atop the same grubby and flattened pillows. The same old dirty blankets wrapped around her like a warm, comforting embrace. She inhaled deeply, breathing in the familiar and nostalgic smell of cigarettes, stale alcohol and sweat. It was almost comforting, in a way. But there wasn't anything new or different about the bed itself; it was Ash's desire for revenge that had changed.

Ash's phone, which was laying on the bedside table, lit up with a ping. She groaned as she reached for it. A message from Kat in the "Maple Hospital Department Managers" group chat, which read;

"Good afternoon. Doctor Anderson has arranged an urgent meeting at his office at 4:45 PM. All members must attend, otherwise will be demoted."

Ash scoffed at Kat's threat, before reality hit her like a ton of bricks; she realized this meeting wasn't just any regular meeting. This was about Quinn's murder.

"Shit!" Ash exclaimed as she literally tumbled out of bed and raced into the shower. She had to look at least somewhat presentable for the unexpected meeting, especially after being gone from the hospital for so long. After her shower, she hurriedly threw on her maroon-coloured scrubs and a badge which read, "Ash Thomas - Administration of Nursing." She then raced out of the house, careening down the street to the hospital.

For most staff, walking through the hospital entrance was simply the beginning of another busy shift, but for Ash, it was a traumatic journey down a difficult memory lane. Every step brought back another memory of the hell that both Ash and her daughter went through in those few nightmarish days. Memories of the day that she had brought Ellie into the hospital in a terrified worry, memories of the chaos that ensued during the worst days of Ash's existence, and memories of the devastating day that Ash left the hospital, alone.

Driven by her rising feelings of unease, Ash hurried to the office, arriving only 4 minutes late. Upon entering, she found every department manager seated around the table in stillness. The moment she opened the door, she caught an awkward glimpse of Emma, who also happened to be in attendance, despite not being a department manager.

Ash couldn't help but wonder about Emma's presence at the meeting. Did Emma replace Quinn as the head doctor? It wouldn't have been a likely scenario since she's only a nurse, and Ash suspected Rosa would've been selected for that position. As she pondered all the possibilities, one realization struck: Emma was the one who found Quinn's deceased body.

There was a churning sensation in Ash's stomach as she sat down, a silent prayer on her lips that her theory was incorrect. Out of all the people in the world, anyone but Emma... Regardless of only knowing her for a few months, Ash was well aware that someone as delicate as Emma would be unable to process the horrors of discovering such a gore scene. Emma's tears, however, only served to cement Ash's belief that her theory was indeed correct.

"Good evening, Ash," Anderson greeted her warmly, opening the door and offering her a seat. As she sat opposite Kat, Ash felt a palpable unease in the room. Everyone was silent, avoiding eye contact with one another, which only added to the mounting tension.

"As I was saying," Anderson continued as if Ash had never walked in, "we must address the situation at hand. Unfortunately, earlier today, we discovered the tragic passing of our fellow doctor, Doctor Nia Quinn."

A small, stunned gasp escaped from the mouths of the small audience, including Ash's own. She glanced over to see a single tear running down Emma's face.

Despite the thick, oppressive atmosphere of grief and sadness surrounding the room, Ash did not feel a shred of regret, remorse, or guilt. If anything, the sight of everyone else mourning for their loss only reinforced her own sense of achievement. To her, an eye for an eye was merely a fair trade, and a life for a life was a simple, acceptable exchange, one that she had no intention of feeling any shame or contrition for.

"Doctor Neil David from the Pathology department has some more information on the situation," Anderson continued calmly.

As David stood up to speak, Ash felt her heart begin to beat at a faster pace, her adrenaline and nerve mixed together in a torrent of emotion.

"Unfortunately, this was a murder." Ash's heart almost jumped out of her chest hearing this statement. She knew that Quinn's body would quickly be discovered, but not *this* quickly.

"The destruction on her face made it clear to see that she was brutally attacked by a heavy object, which we suspect was a hammer or something similar."

Ash couldn't help but notice the intense stare that Kat was giving from opposite her. This only made her feel even more anxious, causing her to fidget with her hands in distress.

David continued to explain the situation. "So far, we have no evidence or suspects, but my team of pathologists are currently doing an autopsy. Fingers crossed we'll be able to find some sort of evidence, which will then lead us to the killer."

Ash couldn't help but consider the possibility of going to prison. The thought did not bother her, for every waking day felt like a never-ending prison sentence, a cruel punishment for a life spent in solitude. Even the possibility of receiving the death sentence failed to elicit a reaction, as she had not a person or reason to live for. The only solace she could find was in the thought that if she were executed, her isolated suffering would finally come to an end.

Ash was completely aware of the consequences of her actions, but pondering them was like engaging in an invigorating game. Numerous unanswered queries lingered in the air, each one more captivating than the last. Could they uncover any incriminating evidence? Would anyone ever suspect her of being the perpetrator? Only one question stood above the rest, one that commanded all of her attention. How many unsuspecting victims could she murder before they discovered her true identity?

"Do you have any CCTV footage of the murder?" Surgeon Wilson - Administration of Surgery – inquired.

Anderson responded, "Unfortunately, no. We are having new CCTV cameras installed this week; therefore, we haven't captured any evidence. Additionally, the area where the murder occurred is not covered by CCTV."

Kat clicked her clicky-pen before suggesting, "I think it would be beneficial for us to note what everyone was engaged in this morning so that we may establish potential links to help uncover the ruthless perpetrator. Let's begin with Ash."

All of a sudden, the eyes of every individual in the room trained on Ash, as if examining her every move, every sentence, every detail. She felt the air grow colder as anxiety surged through her veins. In order to regain control of herself, she took a deep breath and replied in a blunt and emotionless tone, "I spent the morning on the phone with a crematorium service, discussing Ellie's cremation costs. And then I agonized over what of Ellie's belongings I would discard and what I would keep."

Everyone in the meeting cast uncomfortable glances away in discomfort.

"Thank you, Ash," Anderson swiftly interrupted, being aware that Ash had no desire to open up about her day.

While everyone else in the meeting discussed their false suspicions and speculations, Ash remained silently seated at the end of the table, observing as everyone else talked. At this point, she couldn't help but be filled with jealousy as she watched Rosa comfort Emma at the other end of the room. While desperately craving this comforting care, Ash knew deep down that someone who is as flawed and sinful as herself would not deserve such a luxury.

As the conclusion for the meeting was soon reached, individuals began to slowly rise from their seats. However, Kat remained seated, continuing to fix her gaze intently on Ash. Was her attention some type of warning? Or was she simply attempting to irritate Ash like she does with so many others? Feeling the pressure of the situation, she chose to ignore it and quickly left the meeting.

5:32 PM

Ash hurried along the long, dim hospital aisle, completely immersed in thought as she planned her next killing spree. Her gruesome ideas were abruptly shattered by a clicking sound that was becoming increasingly louder with each step. Once she quickly turned to face the source, she saw Kat approaching. As soon as they locked eyes, Kat accused, "You did it, didn't you."

Ash's heart quickened as she thought about being caught. In a desperate attempt to maintain her composure, she asked, "What?"

Kat grew closer and closer, her expression remaining tense. "You killed her," the younger woman whispered, before growing louder and insisting, "Admit it, Ash. You killed her."

Kat's taunting voice continued to shadow her as she tried to walk away, repeating the same questions in a persistent manner. Ash's rage grew with each word, prompting her to rush to the janitor's closet in order to avoid the questioning.

"You killed Quinn because you're too irresponsible, incompetent, and lousy of a mother to care for your own child," the cruel voice rang through Ash's ears. Although she remained expressionless, Ash flinched at the brutal words, her entire body began tensing as Kat pushed her to her very last nerve.

"Instead of accepting the fact that you are incapable and irresponsible enough to properly care for your daughter, you take your grief out on innocent individuals, like a sadistic devil. Deprived of happiness and devoid of a will to exist."

Ash's eyes widened as her jaw locked in place, feeling shocked at how accurate Kat's words were.

"You have no right to call yourself a mother. A mother should protect and cherish her children, and you failed at doing both." Kat continued. While Ash was hurt to admit it, the very core of her being could not refute the truthfulness of Kat's statements. She truly had no right to call herself a mother.

Moving slowly and cautiously, Ash pivoted to face Kat, her words still ringing in her ears. Her jaw clenched and teeth ground together as she seethed, "How dare you," while trying to control herself. Clenched fists pressed tightly against her sides, Ash took a deep breath and attempted to regain control of her anger. However, that rage was palpable, and her voice commanded and carried a threat of physical violence.

Kat took a step back, her eyes wide with fear. She had pushed Ash too far and realized that something terrible was about to happen to her. She frantically searched the room for something to protect herself, but it was all too late. With sudden fury, Ash let out a howling roar and charged forward in Kat's direction. A brutal punch landed with intense force and Kat was sent careening to the ground, crying out with pain.

Rosa and Emma stood outside the director's office after the end of the meeting, with a feeling of tension and suspense in the air. Rosa looked at Emma reassuringly and asked, "Will you be alright tonight, Gem?" Her gentle voice was filled with concern and worry, as she was aware of the difficult position that Emma was in.

Emma nodded faintly and forced a light smile on her face. "I'll be alright." Despite the dreadful day she had, the sound of Rosa's soft voice as she called Emma "Gem" brought a warm feeling to her heart. It reminded her of the day they met, when Emma's name was unknown to Rosa. Emma's aquamarine gemstone necklace – a good luck gift from her parents, caught Rosa's eye, leading her to nickname her "Gemstone necklace girl." The name had now been shortened to Gem, symbolizing a constant reminder of how much Rosa cares and appreciates her.

With a sigh, Rosa replied, "If you say so..." Then she added, with a smile: "If you need anything, just call me, okay?"

A brief moment of silence followed before Rosa continued, "Anyway, I must be on my way. Daniel is waiting for me at home."

At the mention of his name, Emma perked up and raised an eyebrow in surprise. In response, she asked, "Daniel? Doctor Daniel Graham?"

Rosa smiled in response. "Yeah, we've been getting along pretty well lately."

Emma squints her eyebrows in confusion and asks, "Are you guys like a couple now?"

Rosa, visibly uncomfortable, responds swiftly, "No, not at all!" A slight tremble in her voice indicates her unease as she avoids eye contact and fiddles with the ring on her index finger. After this, she finishes hastily with, "He's coming over to fix a leaking pipe, that's all!" She ended the conversation with a haste and says, "Anyway, I must be going! See you tomorrow, Gem."

The office fell silent as Rosa made her exit. Her sudden mention of Daniel caught Emma's attention, her curiosity piqued at the idea of her best friend and Daniel becoming a couple. Despite not sounding utterly convincing, Emma has a lot of trust for Rosa, so she took her word. Besides, they are best friends, with Emma always being the first to know about everything going on in Rosa's life.

However, there was still something that felt off in their interaction, leading Emma to trust her instinct by keeping an eye on Daniel. Regardless, she decided to take a moment to clear her head and move on with her day. With a final sigh, she left the office, finally ready to go home and close the curtains on this hellish day once and for all.

As Emma walked down the hallway, a strange, muffled sound coming from the janitor's closet caught her attention. Emma was intrigued and began to approach it. As she drew closer, she noticed that the sound became louder. Despite its muted and obscure nature, it caught her attention, leading her to take note of it. Nonetheless, the mystery behind the curious sound continued to deepen as she got ever closer to the source.

Pinned next to the janitor's closet door, Emma couldn't contain her sheer curiosity and started to listen carefully to the unusual sounds within. The muffled grunts and apparent straining of flesh made for a disturbing backdrop, only enhanced by her heart's rapid beat. As she placed her ear up against the door, the ominous silence only further heightened her feeling of unease. She couldn't help but consider the possibility that her imagination was running wild due to her heightened emotions.

In a panic, Emma stood in the hallway, deliberating what course of action to take. Flashbacks from earlier in the day prevented her from entering the janitor's closet, but numerous thoughts continued to run through her mind. Should she investigate the sound or ignore it? Perhaps it was just the washing machines? Or was someone getting attacked? As the seconds passed, she realized that if her suspicions were true, she needed to act quickly to find the truth.

After the door slammed shut, Emma stood in shock and horror at the sight before her. She couldn't believe what she was seeing. Kat lying unconscious on the floor, a bruised face and slight smudge of blood on her lower cheek, along with Ash straddled on top of Kat with her hands around her throat.

As Emma stood, paralyzed by the horrific scene before her, her heart pounded at an alarming rate, her body trembling in fear and panic. The steady dripping of sweat down her face seemed to mirror the tight, aching pain within her chest, as if her body was a reflection of her racing thoughts. She felt as though she was trapped in a suspended animation, unable to act or process what was unfolding before her eyes. Her breathing became laboured as she realized she wasn't staring at a murder; she was *witnessing* a murder.

Emma knew she had to do something, but what? She couldn't just stand there and watch. She had to help Kat. But how? She couldn't take on Ash by herself. She needed a plan.

In a moment of quick thinking, Emma grabbed a nearby mop and swung it at Ash's head. Ash flinched at the impact, releasing her grip on Kat's throat.

Emma gazed down at Kat's wounded body, waiting anxiously for a gasp of air to come from her mouth. It was at that moment that she realized; *it was too late.*

Ash held the top of her head, groaning in pain as she stared at Emma.

"Did you just hit me with a fucking mop?"

The coldness in her eyes as she ignored the body beside her suggested a person who was completely indifferent to what had just happened. It was as if the murder, and its violent and gruesome consequences, meant absolutely nothing to her, almost as if it were a completely ordinary occurrence.

"Y-You were strangling her!" Emma stuttered, with the mop still in hand. "What else was I supposed to do?! You were killing an innocent soul!"

"Not hit me with a mop, idiot!" Ash snatched the mop from Emma's hand. The slight force caused Emma to fall to the ground. Ash rolled her eyes, as if annoyed by the fact that she had to explain herself. "She was no innocent soul," Ash replied, her tone still devoid of emotion. "She was a threat."

Fear still gnawed at Emma's heart, and she could feel her pulse pounding in her ears as she looked at Ash, trying to process the situation. But Ash's coldness and lack of emotions made it difficult to think straight.

"Listen here, Emma." Ash suddenly grabbed the top of Emma's blue scrubs, before aggressively pulling her closer. "Don't you dare speak a word of this to anyone. You wouldn't want to end up like her, would you? I know you've seen what I've done, but I'm offering you a chance to protect everything you hold, Dear. Don't waste it."

Ash's dominance almost felt mind controlling. Emma found herself listening to Ash's every word.

"Don't mistake my silence for ignorance, for I could make your life fall apart with a few words. I may be a grieving mother, but I am also a killer, and I will stop at nothing to protect myself. Got it?"

Emma felt like she was drowning in a pool of fear and uncertainty. She couldn't bear the thought of putting her loved ones in harm's way, but she also couldn't bring herself to lie to the grieving mother. She was trapped between a rock and a hard place, and she wasn't sure how to get out.

"Got it?!" Ash repeated, in a louder and even more dominating tone.

"G-Got it…" Emma whispered. The fear on Emma's face confirmed to Ash that she took every word seriously. Ash let go of her grip with a slight push, then stood up and smirked evilly, relishing the fact that Emma had just made this game even more thrillingly exciting.

"Meet me at my house tomorrow morning. Don't think about not listening to me, or there will be consequences. Now, get out of here and go home."

Chapter 4
Puppet on a string.

Monday, January 9th, 8:46 AM.

A small house with walls faintly painted blue, a dirty garage to the left, a window with closed curtains, and a white door. House number 23 on Hazel Street. Ash's house.

Emma watched the steamy fog escape her mouth with each deep breath that she took to steady her racing heart. Perhaps she was making a huge mistake that could end in her own murder. Or, she could convince Ash to put an end to this disastrous madness. Emma clutched her bag and keys tightly and anxiously approached the front door, feeling unsure of what she would find on the other side.

3 knocks.

As expected, Ash opened the door. "Good morning, Ash," said Emma, forcing a friendly smile despite the anxiety and regret that simmered just beneath the surface. Ash's lips curved upward in a faint smile in response. "Good morning. Come in, it's cold."

Emma took a seat on the warn out couch, before Ash called from the kitchen, offering her a drink as she brewed herself a coffee.

"No, thanks," Emma replied, her gaze scanning the room and taking in its odd scents, cigar-stained curtains, and the childish stickman drawing of a family of two drawn with markers on the wall: proof that a young child had once lived there.

As she looked to the left, Emma found a scruffy, blue notebook with its sides ragged and damaged with a cover that was creased. Curiosity got the better of her, and she wondered, *'What could be inside a cold-blooded psychopath's notebook?'*

She picked it up, looking around to make sure Ash wasn't nearby. Nothing written in the notebook could compare to the atrocious carnage she had seen in the last forty-eight hours.

She turned the cover, revealing the first page, which was a list. At the top of the list was her co-worker's name, Nia Quinn, crossed out in black ink. Underneath the name were others she'd never heard of, including Charlie Smith and Esther Lewis, followed by Kat Parker, which was also crossed out, Daniel Graham, Joel Anderson... and Emma Middleton. Her own name. Written on a list that consisted of two crossed-out murder victims.

Before Emma could even process what she was seeing, Ash appeared behind her. "Put that down," she demanded in a dry, expressionless voice.

Her sudden appearance caused Emma to jump. "What is this?!" she exclaimed, raising her voice.

"Why are you looking through my things?"

"Are you going to kill me?!"

"If I were going to kill you, I would've done it by now."

Though Ash's words were blunt, there was no denying the cold, intimidating tone that accompanied them. It sent an uncomfortable chill down Emma's spine, leaving her feeling exposed and vulnerable. An uncomfortable silence fell between them, the atmosphere heavy with tension.

Emma finally found her voice. "About last night," she started, eager for answers. Ash's face lit up immediately, recognizing what Emma was referring to. Without any ounce of guilt, she casually admitted to killing Quinn.

"Why?!" Emma's voice rose as she let out a stream of questions. Still, what Ash revealed to her came as no surprise, given what she had personally witnessed the previous night.

Ash's voice sounded like a cold, sharp blade, cutting through the air and striking Emma with a cutting precision. "Because she killed my daughter."

Emma's voice trembled as she looked up at Ash, trying to understand the raw emotion behind her words. "You know it wasn't on purpose," she stammered.

Ash looked up, meeting Emma's eyes with a blank expression, as if killing was nothing more than a minor annoyance. "I know," she said, her voice devoid of emotion. "But I had to. She promised that Ellie would've been okay," she continued while staring into her coffee. Since Ellie's passing, Ash had become an emotionless creature, unable to express her emotions.

"But why Kat?!" Emma demanded. "She's done nothing to you!"

"She suspected that I murdered Quinn," Ash continued, as if killing was no more than a minor annoyance. "It wouldn't be any fun if the game ended before it even started, would it not?"

Emma's anger rose like a blazing fire. "Are you serious? Is this just some silly little game to you?!" she cried, her fists clenching in frustration.

Ash's eyes widened with delight, her face brightening up with a smile of excitement. "Yes, exactly that!" she declared with a glint of glee in her eyes. "It's a game of thrills, secrets and excitement, all with the risk of being caught!"

Hearing Ash call Quinns death a mere 'game' was like a painful stab to the gut, bringing back vivid flashbacks as if it had happened 5 minutes ago. Emma was frozen in shock once more, breathing rapidly as the flashbacks attacked her mind. She remembered the nauseating scene so vividly: Quinns's cold, stiff, grey body, which was covered in a thick, dark, red coat of blood. Her eyes remained white, resembling the clouds above in colouring.

Emma stared at the coffee table in front of her like she was time travelling to the day she found her friend's bloodied body. The pungent aroma of blood was almost present in the air, and its wintery bite could almost be felt on her face. The sound of Ash's malicious voice however pulled her back into reality with chilling effect.

"And now you're going to play along." Ash sneered.

Emma was taken aback. "What?!" she sputtered, feeling as if Ash was mocking her loss. Ash's smirk remained unscathed, as if she had no regard or empathy for anyone but herself.

"You're the perfect partner," Ash continued. "You're naïve, gullible, and susceptible. These factors will let me guide and protect you."

Emma was taken aback by Ash's cold and calculated demeanour. Her words about Emma being "naïve, gullible, and susceptible" echoed in her ears, causing her to question her own abilities and judgement.

'Guide and protect me?' she thought. *'Is this some kind of sick joke?'* She felt a sudden chill rush down her spine. What was Ash trying to say? Was she planning on taking advantage of her?

"I... I don't trust you," she muttered, her gaze uncomfortably fixed on the floor.

There was a hint of menace in Ash's eyes. "It's just a bit of fun, Emma," she said, her voice carrying a sinister layer underneath the casual demeanour. "You can trust me," Ash's expression changed, her smirk fading into a cold stare "And if you refuse, *you will be my next victim.*"

Emma's emotions were running wild, raging all the way from fury to fear and everything in between. The realization that she had walked straight into Ash's trap was overwhelming, she couldn't process what was happening. Everything was happening so fast; she couldn't shake the feeling that her time was running out. The fear that had been brewing inside her for so long was finally boiling over, she was completely powerless. Her mind wanted to lash out, scream, cry, and somehow make Ash pay for what she had done, but Emma knew that she couldn't. She was trapped in Ash's twisted game, and there was no way out.

She couldn't refuse to help Ash – if she did, she would be killed within a second. If she accepted her fate, she would become a harbinger of death. The thought of having Ash end her life within an instant was almost appealing compared to the thought of aiding her in the death of innocent lives, but it still terrified Emma.

The memory of Quinn's state was haunting, and she couldn't imagine how excruciating such a violent death would be. And to know that one wrong move would put her in the same situation was beyond terrifying, beyond words.

And yet, as Ash's cold eyes met hers, Emma felt as if she had no choice but to play along. Ash's words had a mesmerizing effect on her, as if casting a spell that made her feel completely powerless. All she could do was hope, beg, that she would survive this game, and that maybe, just maybe, she would find a way to make Ash pay for what she had done.

"You're evil." Emma murmured as feelings of rage, hopelessness and defeat took over her.

"I'm not evil, Emma. I'm human." Ash replied. "Humans are no different than any other living creature. A lion will take down its prey, and a bear will defend her young. Death is a part of nature, and to deny that is to deny the law of the jungle."

The silence that followed was heavy, as if it was a living entity, slowing down time with the sole purpose of causing Emma discomfort. Ash's sudden question caught Emma off guard, and she could feel the tension in the air.

"Don't you ever feel the desire to kill those who have caused you pain and suffering?" Ash asked, her question cutting through the silence like a knife, as if she were killing the silent entity.

Emma was shocked at both the question and the way in which Ash casually asked it. She couldn't believe what she was hearing. Sure, she had felt intense hatred before, but never to the point of wanting to hurt anyone. But Ash seemed surprised, as if it was a normal thing for someone to want revenge.

"Not at all?" Ash asked. "You mean you've never felt the desperate desire for revenge?"

Emma remained quiet. She had never dreamt of hurting a fly, let alone killing another human being. But there was no point in arguing with Ash, she knew that she would only manipulate her into questioning her beliefs.

"There's bound to be someone you don't like. Take Daniel Graham for example." Ash continued, as if this was a justification for killing. "He's selfish and disloyal," she added, as if that was reason enough to kill him.

"That doesn't mean he deserves to die," Emma cried.

"You really think everyone deserves to live, even me?"

"Yes!"

"Even Jeffrey Dahmer? Terrorists?" Ash scoffed.

Emma hesitated for a moment, but then replied, "Y-yes…?"

"Damn," Ash snorted. "Maybe you're more fucked up than I am."

"Okay… Well, I better get going." said Emma, standing up and gathering her belongings. "I'll see you later."

As she stepped outside, she noticed a light blue Sudan car parked in front of another nearby house. It was Rosa's car, but what was she doing there at this early hour? Emma squinted her eyes, straining to get a better look at the two people emerging from the house. Her heart pounded as she recognized Rosa, and next to her was Daniel. The two shared a kiss and a tight hug before Rosa walked to her car, with Daniel waving goodbye.

Emma stood frozen, staring blankly at the pair as Rosa drove off. Her heart broke less from the fact that Rosa was with someone else and more from the fact that Rosa had kept it from her.

She doesn't believe that anybody 'belongs' to anyone, but Rosa is *hers*. Not in a sense that she 'owns' Rosa, but they will always have each other no matter what the world throws at them. They're like the sun and the moon, the yin and the yang, the salt and the pepper. Through Emma's eyes, she's the vase, and Rosa is the beautiful Rose which fills her emptiness, which is secretly the reason why Emma nicknamed her 'Rose.'

Their friendship is not one where falsehoods lie upon. It's a friendship of honesty, respect and trust. To lie felt like a betrayal. Emma wanted to know anything there was to know about her dear friend, including the things Rosa felt she should keep hidden.

Still standing in one place, Emma wondered *'Why?'* Out of all the men in the world, why Daniel? The one man whose known for his disloyal actions, infidelity, and greed. Rosa is bound to end up hurt. Emma could not risk that. Not Rosa, the kindest heart on this planet could not hurt. In order to protect Rosa from Daniel's evilness, she must get rid of him. But how…?

Emma ran back into the house and slammed the front door behind her, catching Ash's attention. "I've changed my mind." she stated, her determination to stop Rosa from getting hurt, even if it meant doing something bad, was apparent. *"Let's fucking get him."*

"Gone." Doctor Joel Anderson whispered under his breath, staring down at the deceased body of someone he once knew. "Forever gone…" He took Kat's cold, stiff hand, who was lying on the metal autopsy table. "I'm so sorry it ended for you this way, my sweet Kat." He cried, bringing the woman's hand to his chest. "Whoever did this to you will pay…"

Doctor David gently placed his hand on the grieving man's back. "I know how hard it is to lose someone special, Joel."

Completely ignoring his friend's attempt at reassurance, Anderson squeezed his hands into fists. "I'll find that bastard even if it's the last thing I do!" The older man turned to look at his friend with demanding eyes. "Tell me everything, EVERYTHING you know!"

David began explaining the redness around Kat's neck, suggesting that she was attacked and strangled, and the small wounds covering the lady's face further proved his point. "Although, usually an attack would result in more wounds…"

Anderson suggested that the murderer must have stopped attacking Kat when they realized the bloody wounds would leave a mess, to which David agreed. "That could be the case," he said. "Kat's body was discovered this morning. It was cold, suggesting that she was attacked at some point last night, possibly after the meeting."

The two men stood in silence for a moment as they thought about the night before, trying to refresh their minds on what everyone was doing. That's when David remembered seeing Kat quickly exit the staff room, chasing after a black-haired woman. The same black-haired woman that was late to the meeting. "I may have an idea…"

"What?!" Ash exclaimed, taken aback by Anderson's accusation. "How on earth could you even think that I would do something like that, especially after the loss of my own child? Do you think I would want to put someone through the same pain I'm feeling?!"

Anderson raised his eyebrows in sudden surprise as he leaned back in his chair, embarrassed with the realization that he accused Ash without any concrete evidence. "You're completely right, Ash." He admitted. "My apologies. I let my emotions get the best of me. Please accept my most sincere apologies for any pain I have caused you."

Ash nodded, finally calmed down. "It's alright." She spoke warmly. "I understand that you're upset and frustrated. After losing my own daughter, I can confidently say that death is an evil curse sent by the devil himself. It's a pain that no one should ever have to endure."

Anderson's face softened as he offered a grateful smile. "Thank you for understanding, Ash. Before you leave, could you please keep this case quiet? We don't want to risk the murderer finding out that we're investigating them. And if you could, please send Emma to my office."

With a nod, Ash turned towards the door, where a sly, evil smirk crept across her face.

Sold.

As Emma frantically waited for Ash to exit the office, she imagined the worst-case scenario. *'What if Joel found out about Kat? Would I be blamed for not saving her on time?'*

Her heart sank as Ash emerged from the office with a smirk on her face. "Fancy seeing you here," Ash said, but her tone quickly switched to a frown.

"Is everything okay?!" Emma panicked. "Why did he call you in? Are you in trouble?"

"Everything is fine." Ash uttered coldly. "He wants to see you."

Emma's body instantly tightened up. Her shoulders pulled back, her face frozen with worry. She began to fidget with the clicky-pen in her pocket, the only thing that helped her to ground herself when she was in a state of high stress such as this one.

The older woman raised an eyebrow at Emma as she watched her reaction. "Don't work yourself up," she grunted, clearly sick of Emma's constant worries and wanting her to calm down and handle things like a mature adult. "It's not like he's going to believe you if you let the truth sweat off your head! It would be much easier for the both of us if you didn't act so pathetic."

After quickly glancing around the room to check if no one was coming, she grabbed Emma's shirt and dragged her to the side. Placing both her hands on Emma's shoulders, Ash looked straight into her hazel eyes with a piercing gaze.

"Manipulate him," she demanded, completely neglecting Emma's need for reassurance. "Gaslight him, sell him our precious lie, otherwise you'll be in handcuffs and—"

As Ash was about to continue her lecture, the door just behind the two women leading to the staff toilets swung open. A young woman exited with blonde hair tied up in a tight ponytail and light purple hairband. She wore light purple scrubs and small, studded purple earrings. She had eyes bluer than the ocean and perfectly shaped eyebrows, not a single mark or blemish in sight.

"Hi!" the young girl exclaimed, her voice friendly and energetic as she inquired about Nurse Ash's whereabouts. She had caught them off guard, leaving them confused and rather startled. Both women turned to look at one another, but they were unable to answer the blonde's question because they were still trying to process the unexpected encounter.

"Yes, I'm Nurse Ash," Ash said with a friendly yet professional demeanour. "Can I help you?"

A spark of joy lit in the young woman's eyes. "Oh my god, hi! I'm Charlotte, one of the new med students!"

"I thought you guys didn't start until April." Ash replied.

"Yeah, but we started early because of the lack of staff. New year, new start, right?!"

Emma let out a fake laugh with an awkward smile. "Right... Erm, I'm going to go, don't want to keep the old man waiting...!"

With Emma gone, Ash was left alone with the young med student Charlotte.

"So, when do we start?!" Charlotte asked giddy with excitement. Ash looked around the room quickly, struggling to come up with an excuse to leave the woman. "Uh...We actually have to wait a bit. It might be a while."

Luckily, Doctor Daniel Graham had just walked into the room, which prompted Ash to call him over. "Daniel, can you take this student for a moment?" Ash called out, and Daniel escorted the student away.

Ash breathed a deep sigh of relief, suddenly finding herself alone and grateful for the opportunity. Now was her chance to get to the basement and complete her exciting plan.

12:45 PM. Perfect.

3 hours earlier...

Emma's raging fire had dwindled into a quiet ember as her anger cooled into regret. She quietly muttered to herself, "I... I don't know if I want to do this anymore…"

Ash paused her writing and lifted her head. "Do you care about Rosa or not?" she asked bluntly.

Emma hesitated briefly before responding. "Of course, I love her," she said softly, but Ash quickly interrupted. "Do you want her to get hurt?"

Emma fell silent, her resolve temporarily shattered as she realized that Ash was right. "No…" the brunette mumbled, "But…"

Ash shook her head, adamant in her position. "Then prove it. Don't be a fool. Save her from getting her heart broken."

Emma sat silently, processing Ash's words and realizing that this really might be her only option.
"Surely there has to be a better way…"

Ash promptly shut down Emma's hopeful thoughts. "There is no better way," she said, her voice overflowing with determination. "You need to be strong for yourself, for Rosa. This is the only way to protect her."

Emma's heart raced as the harsh reality sunk in. While the idea of killing Daniel sounded extreme, it would protect Rosa. The older woman's words continued to echo in her mind. This really was the only way to ensure her safety.

But it was wrong.

So, *so wrong.*

And she knew that. But…

There is no greater crime than failing to protect the ones you love.

"Okay. I'll do it," Emma said with a heavy sigh, finally giving into the woman. Ash's face cracked into a small smile, and she let out a quiet mumble of approval. "Good girl," she whispered before returning into her notebook.

"This is the plan," Ash said at last, her voice firm and decisive as she outlined a step-by-step plan. It included the steps needed to gain access to the cyanide, Daniel's daily routine, and how the cyanide would mask its taste in the coffee, among other details.

"Cyanide? Why the hell would the hospital have cyanide?" Emma interrupted, curious about the reason for its presence.

Ash raised an eyebrow. "Don't interrupt me. There was a rat invasion a few weeks ago, so they used it to get rid of them. They kept the spare bottles in case it ever happened again."

"So, you're going to poison him…?" Emma asked, her voice still full of shock at the thought.

Ash's reply came swiftly, without the slightest hesitation. "*We're* going to poison him," she corrected.

"But won't someone notice that the cyanide was taken?" Emma pressed.

Ash looked up again, her voice low and raspy with a villainous smirk on her face. "There's no crime so perfect that it won't leave a clue behind."

Current events

The robotic voice announced, "*Floor 0: Laboratory.*" Ash hid behind the cold, white tiled wall and peaked through the window into the laboratory. She expected to see approximately 3 to 4 medical technologists working, but to her surprise, only one person was present, facing the wall and clearly engaged in work. The staff shortage made it difficult to keep the ideal number of staff present, but it made for a perfect opportunity for Ash to sneak into the laboratory and retrieve the cyanide.

She headed for one of the many storage rooms spread out throughout the hospital and searched for the one that belonged to the laboratory. Inside, it had tall shelves lined with all sorts of books, tools, and chemicals, all cluttered together – one wrong move would cause something to fall. But she didn't have time to get distracted; she was on a mission to find the cyanide, take it, and leave.

After scanning through each shelf, Ash finally found the small bottles labelled "Cyanide – DANGER." They weren't particularly impressive-looking bottles, only smooth glass bottles no larger than her palm. But Ash couldn't ignore the weight of excitement and danger on her shoulders as she reached out to grab one. She was holding a bottle of lethal liquid that would kill her in minutes if she didn't handle it correctly.

Suddenly, she heard a terrifying sound: a rolling bottle followed by a *smash*, then another smash, another smash, and another…

Ash froze in surprise, her heart hammering in her chest as she turned to see the source of the noise.

She had accidentally knocked a book that was sitting too close to the cyanide, knocking the rest of the cyanide bottles off the shelf and sending shards of glass flying in every direction.

"*Shit.*"

As she gazed at the mess, panic took over her body, freezing her in place. This was dangerous. *Extremely dangerous.*

Ash snapped herself out of her panic and forced herself to stop breathing. She quickly jumped off the stool, avoiding the poisonous mess underneath her feet. She ran as quickly as she could to the elevator, finally taking a deep breath when the metal doors shut tight.

Her heart pounded in her chest, but it was unclear whether the adrenaline-fueled rush derived from narrowly escaping death or from something unrelated.

Three loud beeps from the pager clipped to her scrubs brought Ash's focus away from the cyanide. She unclipped the pager and read the message: "**Paediatric Unit, Bed 12, new cannula needed. Patient stable, no urgency.**"

"Crap." Ash muttered, considering her options. She had planned on sneaking the cyanide into her handbag and getting back to work, as it wasn't urgent. However, she suddenly realized that being there so late might raise suspicion. And, what if the cyanide leaked in her bag?

"*Fuck it*," she mumbled under her breath before pressing the 'Floor 2' button on the elevator and quickly returning the cyanide to her pocket.

"I'll deal with it later," she told herself, hoping to ease her mind a bit.

As the elevator lurched into motion, she tried to calm herself down, but her thoughts were still racing, just as her breath and her heart rate. Should she make up an excuse for being there so late? What if someone saw her leaving the elevator with the cyanide in her hand? '*Shit, shit, shit.*'

She tried to take slow, deep breaths, but her chest felt tight and heavy. A sense of panic took over, and her thoughts seemed distorted and blurry. She couldn't tell if she was feeling anxious or if she had inhaled some of the cyanide. Either way, she couldn't afford anyone to raise any suspicion, so she closed her eyes and ignored it, focusing on the job ahead.

Emma walked over to the new patient with Charlotte. "Do you have the documents Graham gave you for handover?" she asked, but Charlotte's cocky reply threw her off.

"Yeah, of course I do. You think I'm gonna' mess up on my first day or something? Geez."

Before Emma could say anything, Ash entered the ward. "What do we have here?" she asked, approaching the patient. Charlotte's demeanour instantly changed when she heard Ash's voice.

"Hello, Ash!" she greeted with excitement.

As Ash walked towards the bed, Emma began explaining. "This is Evelyn-"

"--6-year-old female, Evelyn Jenkins, suffering with Acute pancreatitis. Other symptoms include sinus tachycardia, tachypnoea, nausea and abdominal pain." Charlotte abruptly interrupted and shoved the medical documents in Ash's face.

Emma gave Charlotte an annoyed look, silently cursing her for interrupting her before she could finish her explanation.

"Thank you." Ash replied as she skimmed through the files Charlotte handed to her. "Medical history?"

"Non—"

"Non-contributory."

Ash turned her glance to Emma and found her glaring at Charlotte as the two fought for dominance over the conversation. It reminded her of two siblings bickering after an argument, with each one trying to get the last word.

Ash glared back at the young patient, whose dark brown hair highlighted her hazel eyes and pale skin, along with a nasal cannula wrapped around her face.

Ash leaned down towards the patient. "Hi there, Evelyn!" she said with a friendly tone. "My name is Nurse Ash and I'm here to put a little tube called a canula into your hand. Shall we get started?"

The girl shyly nodded, whispering with a soft, nervous voice, "I'm cold..."

"Charlotte," Ash quickly said, "please grab a spare blanket from the storage room."

As Charlotte fetched the blanket, Emma looked at Ash with a questioning eyebrow raise, indicating that she was asking, "Did you get it?" without speaking. Ash instantly understood the gesture and replied with a confident nod. "I've got it."

Charlotte quickly re-entered the room and handed the blanket to Ash. "Got it!" She said with a proud smile.

Wrapping the blanket around the child, Ash quickly noticed how sick she was. The tubes wrapped around her face, her pale skin, it was almost like a sight she had seen before.

Ellie.

Emma stood at the end of the bed, a tray full of medications in her hands, "The medication is ready. Shall we begin?"

Charlotte stood beside her; her eyes fixed on Emma with an intimidating stare. "Is it really necessary that three people need to give one child a cannula?"

"Actually, as I'm currently working towards my children's nursing degree, Ash is mentoring both of us." Emma explained.

Charlotte rolled her eyes and mumbled "Whatever, let's just begin." Under her breath.

Soon later, the procedure was all done. Emma turned to the patient with a friendly tone, "See, it wasn't that bad, was it?"

"You did great!" Ash said with a comforting smile. Evelyn smiled back at the women, but it quickly faded as she let out a sudden groan.

"Owww, my stomach..." she whined, clutching her abdomen.

"Perhaps we should give her some pain medication." Charlotte suggested.

"According to her records, Doctor Graham already gave her 500 milligrams of acetaminophen," Ash replied. "Adding more could be harmful to a young child, the medication should kick in soon, though."

"In that case, I'm off for my break!" said Charlotte, waving as she exited the ward.

Beep. Beep. Beep.

"Already?!" Ash exclaimed as she looked down at her beeping pager, surprised that she's already being called to another patient. Emma did the same to her beeping pager, which read; "ICU, Room 4 - Urgent. Possible cyanide poisoning. Unstable, on life support"

Emma instantly looked up at Ash. Noticing the 'cyanide poisoning' entry on her own pager. While the chances of a patient coming in with cyanide poisoning wasn't impossible, the fact that it's after Ash grabbed the cyanide from the basement worried Emma. And the way Ash's face suddenly turned pale only added to Emma's worries.

"Ash." Emma spoke as she turned to face Ash, her voice stern. *"What have you done."*

Ash and Emma proceeded to the ICU, and upon arrival, they found Rosa standing outside the room holding two masks.

"Ah, you're here." Rosa said before passing the masks to the women. "Wear these" she said, "for safety reasons."

With the masks on, the three women walked into the room where a young unconscious man was lying in bed.

"This is Justin Miller," Rosa began. "Twenty-eight-year-old male, suspected cyanide poisoning."

After Rosa explained the situation and gave the two nurses orders of what to do next, she exited the room and closed the door behind her.

The moment the door closed, Ash instantly raised a question: "Ash, what the hell happened?!"

Ash didn't seem at all bothered as she answered simply, "When I grabbed the cyanide, a few other bottles fell off the shelf. He probably heard the smash and came to investigate."

Emma began to prepare one of the tasks ordered by Rosa, but not before making a sarcastic comment under hear breath, "Course' you did."

Emma looked up at Emma and asked bluntly, "What are you doing?"

Emma replied without looking up, her eyes fixed on what she was doing. "Fixing the problems you made."

Ash grabbed Emma's shoulder, saying, "Don't bother."

"What, so we should just stand here and wait for a miracle?" Emma asked sarcastically, but this was no joke to her co-worker.

"A miracle won't happen." Ash said seriously as she began to prepare what looked like a saline injection.

"Saline? Seriously?! What's that going to do?!" she asked sarcastically. For a moment, she thought maybe Ash was foolish enough to believe that saline would save the dying man, but of course, Ash had other intentions.

Ash replied calmly, "Kill him."

Emma's look turned blank as Ash cut across and spoke logically. "Don't be an idiot! He's not even as old as me! You can't just kill him. He has a family; he has a life-"

Ash cut across her statement, "Well guess what, he's older than Ellie." She then ordered, "Imagine yourself in his situation, Emma."

A moment of silence passed as Emma stared back at Ash, who continued with a grim reality: "Imagine if he survived. He'd suffer with breathing difficulties, severe health problems, and pain for the rest of his life."

"I want him to live." Emma continued, but her argument quickly began to lose ground.

Ash stood her ground and replied with a logical but stern tone, "But he won't be able to recover. He won't see his family, or his friends again. It's too late."

Ash continued to give Emma a quick rundown of how an air bubble would travel straight to the man's heart, almost instantly killing him. "Let his suffering end." She said as she forcefully placed the needle in Emma's hand and closed her fingers around it.

Emma, facing a dark reality, looked down at the needle and then at the man's face. Would letting him live mean being the bad guy?

Ash stayed silent, but her piercing stare screamed, "*Do it, do it, do it!*" into her ears. Emma's mind had reached its boiling point. The voices in her head arguing over right and wrong were overwhelming.

Emma clenched her eyes shut and pushed the plunger without giving it a second thought, sending both the saline and air on a short journey to the heart, where the man's short, innocent life will come to a peaceful end.

Emma's fear rose rapidly as she gazed at the patient. Her eyes darted between the man, the needle, and the heart monitor. Her heart dropped as the monitor stayed silent and the man did not immediately convulse.

Emma's realization came quickly, however. Ash had unplugged the monitor, stopping it from registering the patient's vitals and his true condition.

As the realization of her actions washed over her, Emma's tear-filled eyes widened. She sat on the chair, holding her mouth shut, and a quiet, muffled cry could be heard between her lips.

"Get up." Ash demanded, her tone growing increasingly cold. "Stop crying. You're a weapon. Weapons don't weep."

After demanding her to pull herself together, Ash took a glance at the clock. Ash spoke quietly as if to herself, "Your shift will be over in a few minutes. Pull yourself together. I'll see you tomorrow."

Chapter 5
Hidden beneath it all

Tuesday, January 10th, 12:00 PM.

Emma's heart pounded as she sat in the director's office. The chair was comfortable enough, yet her anxiety and anticipation made the leather armrests feel slippery and cold under her sweaty palms. The previous summons had been nothing more than a small discussion, but Emma knew this one was different. While Anderson was widely known for his kindness and sympathy, only a few were aware of his sharp and unforgiving side. A side that was rare to encounter, yet one Emma may soon meet.

"Emma…" Anderson sighed. "I'm sure you're already aware why I've called you here today, but in case you don't, I would like to discuss the events from last night, regarding your patient Justin Miller."

Just the mere mention of that name made Emma feel a massive wave of guilt, weighing down every aspect of her mind and body. It was as if a boulder of guilt had been placed on her, making it difficult to even think straight.

"Twenty-eight-year-old man, suspected cyanide poisoning." Anderson read aloud one of the documents opposite him. "The autopsy revealed that he died from an air embolism. I've already called Ash in, and she's explained the entire situation."

Anderson locked his eyes with Emma, his expression was one she'd never seen before. "I understand that you've been feeling on edge recently, and making mistakes is a part of learning. But your mistakes are costing lives, Emma."

'*My mistakes are costing lives…? Just what on earth did Ash tell him?!*'

"Here at this hospital, we save lives, not take them." Anderson's words were laced with anger and his manner changed from a calm discussion to a stern scolding. "Small avoidable mistakes are just not acceptable and cannot be tolerated."

The audible frustration was clear in Anderson's tone, as well as the fact that he was taking his anger out on Emma, rather than calmly discussing the issue as he had described it initially.

The weight of shame rested heavy on Emma's shoulders. She was not accustomed to being in trouble. Despite her best efforts to maintain eye contact with Anderson in a professional manner, she wanted nothing more than to curl up into a ball and disappear.

"As a result of your mistakes, for the safety of our patients, we've decided to temporarily remove your right to give intravenous procedures to patients."

Anderson continued to explain the new boundaries put in place, but Emma could barely listen. The news of her suspension only added to her already overwhelming emotions. She felt guilty for her 'mistake', but the thought of being punished was more than just humiliating – it was devastating, sending her over the edge. Unable to hold back her sobs, she buried her face into her hands and tears flowed down her face.

For a moment, the idea of telling Anderson the truth about Ash crossed Emma's mind. She needed something, just something to put the blame on, otherwise the huge boulder of regret, embarrassment and shame would crush her bones into millions of pieces. But she couldn't bring herself to tell him. The truth, in this instance, would sound too much like a fiction. Anderson would never have believed her. Besides, surely this was better than being murdered by her so-called 'partner', right?

"I-I'm so sorry..." Emma sobbed as she looked up at Anderson, desperately hoping he would accept her apology for making such a major mistake. However, when Anderson only sat there silently and awkwardly, she felt even more mortified. After what seemed like an eternity, Anderson finally passed Emma a tissue and sent her home to rest.

As she made her way down one of the many busy corridors, Emma kept head down, tucked into her coat as she tried to hide her red, swollen eyes from being noticed. She was overwhelmed by her situation. Her mind was clouded with guilt, regret, tears and anger, so much so that a headache started to form. *'But why?'*

She couldn't understand why Ash had to blame it on her in the first place. Why couldn't Ash simply have lied and blamed it on something else?

As wracked with guilt as she was, Emma couldn't help but feel somewhat relieved that she was allowed to go home. She didn't know how she'd deal with Ash and her constant nagging and manipulation. Even the thought of her voice made Emma's blood boil, so much so that she could almost hear Ash's voice calling her name from behind.

"Emma!" A voice called. To Emma's dismay, the voice she had heard in her head wasn't merely imagination. She continued walking, trying to act as if she didn't hear the loud call.

"Where do you think you're going?" Ash shouted again. Emma kept her head down in an attempt to ignore the call.

"Hey, Emma!" Ash finally caught up to her, placing a firm hand on her shoulder and aggressively turning her to face her. "Don't ignore me! What are you doing?"

"Going home." Emma replied flatly, annoyed by Ash's presence. As she spoke, the clear signs of her crying were displayed on her face. Her red and puffy eyes were visible to all, including Ash, who clearly ignored her crying.

"What? So you're just going to leave me here?!"

"Joel called me in, I don't want to deal with any more bullshit."

"Me neither, but I have to stay here for another 6 hours! I would've lost my job if I didn't beg!"

A trio of beeping noises came over Ash's pager. She immediately looked at the page, then back at Emma. "Come to mine later. We need to go somewhere."

Knowing she couldn't refuse without causing more issues, Emma reluctantly agreed. She had no idea what was in store for her at Ash's place, but she could tell it wouldn't be anything positive.

7:00 PM

Ash strolled down the dimly lit aisles with a shopping cart in hand, its wheels rolling silently across the floor. Emma trailed behind, staring up at the towering shelves on either side, filled with various products ranging from breakfast cereals to instant noodles.

"I still don't understand why you've dragged me here." Emma grumbled, still quite annoyed from their earlier encounter.

"I wanted to take you somewhere." Ash replied bluntly as she reached for a box of cornflakes, before tossing it into the cart. She quickly noticed a pink cereal box on the shelf, an overpriced box of plain cereal with pretty pink packaging and a small plastic unicorn toy inside. It was the cereal Ellie would always beg for whenever they went shopping, but the high price made Ash reluctant to purchase it.

Emma knew Ash's attention was on the cereal, and her emotionless face showed even less emotion than usual. Emma quickly suggested changing aisles. "Hey. Ash, mind if we quickly go to the baking isle?"

Ash nodded, and they both made their way to the aisle filled with flour, sugar, countless boxes of cake mix and various other ingredients for baking.

Ash watched as Emma perused the shelves in search of baking supplies. Ash's eyes drifted towards an approaching figure, a younger blonde woman making her way down the same aisle.

"Hide!" Ash whispered, nudging Emma's arm before facing the shelf.

Picking up a strawberry cake mix, Emma looked down the aisle, confused to what Ash was so anxious about. She quickly noticed the same woman and realised why Ash was panicking. "Charlotte? What's she doing here?"

"Quiet, I don't want to talk to her, come on!" Ash nagged as she grabbed Emma's arm and pulled her away. Unfortunately, by this point, Charlotte had already noticed the two women and came racing towards them.

"Oh my god, hi!" Charlotte greeted as she approached them.

"Hey." Emma replied, noticing her shopping cart which was filled with paper plates, napkins, balloons, and various other party food and accessories. Ash didn't pay any attention, instead she stared at the woman in pity.

"Woah, that's… A lot of shopping." said Emma.

"Yeah, it's for my friend's birthday party." Charlotte said with glee. "Her name's April. I'd love to introduce you guys to her!"

When she thought of an idea, her face quickly lit up. "Oh my god, you two should like, definitely come along!"

The two nurses stared at each other hesitantly, before Ash finally spoke up. "We don't have time for parties," She firmly stated.

"Oh, pleaseee?" Charlotte begged. "It would be so much fun, a great way to meet new friends, right? I've invited Rosa and Daniel too!"

The mention of Rosa caught Emma's attention. She wouldn't want to waste any opportunity to be with her dear friend.

"You know, maybe it would be fun." Said Emma, turning to Ash who still stood silently, a look of annoyance on her face.

"We'll think about it," Emma replied as she turned back to Charlotte.

"Great, I hope to see you there!" Before the blonde continued with her shopping, she gave the two women all the information about the party.

Soon after, Ash and Emma also walked away from the isle as they made their way to the warm beverages isle. "About the party..." Emma muttered nervously, but Ash's stern voice cut across. "We're not going."

There was a slight glint of disappointment in Emma's chestnut eyes, but she continued to persuade Ash to change her mind.

"You really think I care about having fun?" Ash snapped angrily, her jaw clenching as Emma nagged about the party.

"But I could—"

"I said no, Emma."

Ash grabbed a jar of instant coffee off the shelf and muttered under her breath, "This will do the trick."

"You're using that? But the hospital already has coffee." Emma asked.

"I'm not poisoning this entire thing, dumbass. That would get the entire staff sick."

Emma tried to ask about Ash's plan, but all she got was a cold response. "Not right now, Emma. We're in public."

After carefully placing the jar of coffee into the cart, Ash finished her shopping by picking up a bouquet of pink and red carnations, lilies, and tulips.

Waiting in the queue to pay for their shopping, Emma tried once more to persuade Ash about the party.

"Ash, give the party another thought. The past few days have been stressful, a break could be good."

This time, though, Ash did not argue. Instead, she sighed in irritation. "Fine. We'll go."

It didn't take Emma long to figure out where Ash wanted to take her. As she stared through the car window, she noticed the large old stone sign with the words 'The Maple Cemetery' engraved in it. Ash parked the car, and they made their way inside of the cemetery, with Ash confidently leading the way. It was clear that this depressing site was a place she had visited many times before.

As the two women walked silently – one determined and the other curious, Emma stared at the hundreds of graves they walked by, some covered with bright, colourful, freshly picked flowers, while others were abandoned with nothing more than years' worth of dirt layered on top of the old stone.

Soon after, Ash came to a pause as the two reached a new gravestone. The black marble surface was marked with a pair of dates and the words:

"Ellie May Thomas - January 17th 2016 – November 25th 2023. My sweet angel, taken too soon, but I'll carry your memory in my heart till' my last breath."

The grave was decorated with pink and purple balloons, slightly deflated from the passage of time. Small rainbow windmills were stuck into the wet ground, pink photo frames filled with a little girl's pictures, along with a damp pink teddy bear and unicorn hairband. Ash leaned down and carefully placed the recently purchased bouquet of flowers into an empty purple vase which sat behind one of the photo frames, before placing a small pink fluffy rabbit plush just in front of it all.

"Happy early birthday, my sweet angel. It breaks my heart that I won't be able to visit you this weekend."

Emma's heart dropped as she heard that sentence. *'Ellie's birthday?'*

Emma's curiosity grew, but she knew better than to interrupt Ash in this moment. The nurse had clearly come to this place to pay respects to someone she loved deeply, and it was not Emma's place to intrude, despite knowing she dragged her there. She let Ash have her moment with Ellie, keeping her questions to herself.

"You would've been 7 years old, isn't that crazy?" she said with a soft smile. "I was actually planning on getting you a bunny rabbit for your birthday, you were begging me for so long. Hopefully bunnies are allowed in heaven, but if not, I've brought you a soft pink bunny teddy instead."

Emma felt almost taken aback as she watched the wholesome interaction between Ash – the grieving, murderous mother, and her daughter's grave. The way she spoke so softly was as if she was having a conversation with a living being in front of her eyes. What baffled Emma the most was seeing how this kind, wholesome mother was hidden beneath Ash's skin all along. Perhaps the woman she faced was not a monster at all, but caring mother who lost herself in the greed for justice.

As Ash stopped talking, Emma decided to raise her voice. "I'm so sorry, Ash... I had no idea it was her birthday so soon."

Ash's voice was soft as she spoke. "It's okay. It would've been on Sunday, but the damn cemetery is closed for maintenance."

"The grave is so beautiful, how often do you come here?" Emma asked.

"As much as I can." Ash replied, her voice still soft as she stared down at the grave, a gentle smile on her face. "It's the closest I get to be to her. She's resting beneath me, but her soul is being protected by God. To be here is the least I can do for her as her mother, but I know she can see me from up above."

Though Emma didn't believe in any religion, hearing Ash continue to talk about how her daughter could hear her words from heaven felt heartwarming. She wondered if such a place existed, then the afterlife might not be so bad after all.

Not long after, Ash stood back up. "We should get going before it gets dark." And the two women left, leaving the souls of the lost to rest.

Thursday, January 12th

The staffroom had a desolate feel to it, with the dim glow of fluorescent lights casting a faint light on the leather sofa that Emma was resting on. Despite the emptiness, the silence of the room was only interrupted by the occasional squish of the leather sofa.

As Emma sunk deeper into the couch, she turned her attention to the clock on the wall. 8:57 PM.

'God, this shift dragged. Only 2 hours to go.'

Night shifts aren't Emma's thing. She would much rather to spend her evening soaking in a hot bubble bath with a glass of wine and chocolate, but here she is, lying on the couch, begging for time to pass by quicker. There was no point in staring at the clock in pity, for she has jobs to do, documents to fill, and schedules to check.

With a sigh, Emma picked up her phone and scrolled through the hospital's schedule, scouring for her name. When she found it, she noticed another entry beneath hers.

"Emma Middleton - Medication Administration, General Ward 2"
"Charlotte Hyle - Medication Administration, General Ward 2"

"I'm working with HER?!" Emma exclaimed to herself. Despite having recently met her, Charlotte seemed nice enough, but the way she constantly interrupted Emma during their first interaction left Emma with lower expectations.

Feeling dejected, Emma forced herself off the couch and took a deep breath, feeling the warm air fill her lungs. Before leaving to make her way to the medicine room, she reminded herself of the upcoming party – something nice to look forward to.

Charlotte quickly turned around when she heard the door creak open, her eyes widening in excitement. However, her expression quickly changed when she noticed the older, brown-haired woman walk into the room.

"Hey, Emma." Said Charlotte with a forced smile.

Emma walks up to the counter where Charlotte is standing, asking, "Have you finished preparing the medications?"

"Yes, except for bed 9 and 10." Charlotte replied as she forced a pill from its packaging, then placing it in a small plastic cup labelled 'Bed 8.'

After skimming through the list of medications, Emma attempted to help Charlotte, but she quickly stopped her.

"I can do it myself!" She said in a childish manner. Emma stepped back and observed without saying anything.

As Charlotte continued to prepare the medications, Emma noticed that she had opened a box of sulfadiazine pills.

'Sulfadiazine? That wasn't on the list...'

Emma quickly realised the error and corrected it. "Careful, Charlotte! Bed 5 needs sulfasalazine, not sulfadiazine." she said as she poured the pills out of the cup. "You really must slow down and ensure that you've read the medication correctly."

"No, I did it right." Charlotte argued.

"No, you didn't. It's difficult to tell, but giving patients wrong medications could be very dangerous!"

While Emma lectured her, Charlotte rolled her eyes in frustration, not wanting to show her embarrassment. "How was I supposed to know?!"

"It's fine, you're a student. Everybody makes mistakes." Emma replied calmly. "Now, please put this in the bin." she said, handing the empty medication packaging to Charlotte.

With a sigh, Charlotte throws the empty packaging into the bin. "You're a lot like Ash, you know." She snapped.

Emma paused. "Excuse me?"

With crossed arms and a stern expression, she said, "You're very bossy and controlling. It's annoying."

While Emma could've lashed out at Charlotte's remarks, she chose to remain professional. Charlotte knows nothing about Ash, and she's simply just being a childish woman, just like how Kat used to be.

"I don't appreciate you calling me that. I am my own person, and I'll never be anything like her." Emma replied.

"Where is she anyway? I wish I was with her." The blonde pouted like a child.

'I wish you were too.' Emma thought to herself, but instead she said, "She doesn't work on Thursdays. Now go give the medications to the *correct* patients."

After a gruelling 45 minutes of hell, it was time for Emma to make her way to the PACU to monitor patients. Luckily, by now, most patients would be asleep, leaving Emma with a nice, quiet, relaxing end to her shift. She strolled down the silent corridors, peeking through the windows to view into the wards.

As she passed the paediatric ward, she decided to have a quick peek through the window to see how Evelyn was doing. She expected the young girl to be fast asleep, but instead, she saw something unexpected. Every child was sleeping peacefully, but Evelyn was wide awake. Worse, next to Evelyn sat Ash.

'Is that Ash? What the hell is she doing?!'

As she watched the two, Emma noticed childish drawings stuck to the wall behind Evelyn, loose crayons spread across the over-bed table, and picture books. For most people, this sight would've been nothing more than a wholesome interaction. But for Emma, it was an uncomfortable sight. As a nurse, Emma knew it was important to maintain a professional barrier between patients, especially paediatric patients, and so this interaction wasn't as sweet as it seemed.

Evelyn quickly noticed the nurse through the window and greeted her with a smile and a wave.

Emma quietly walked into the ward, making sure not to disturb any of the sleeping children.

"Good evening, Evelyn." she said softly. Her eyes turned to Ash, and her expression changed into one of suspicion. "Good evening, Ash."

Although most wouldn't be able to tell, Emma noticed the expression on Ash's face change from unamused to chagrined. Her expressions were almost impossible to tell apart, but Emma had started to understand them, as if she were learning a new language.

"Hi, nurse!" Evelyn exclaimed excitedly.

"Shh, Evelyn. It's late, we don't want to wake up any of your friends, do we." Ash said to the young girl.

"Looks like someone's feeling better." Emma chuckled. "What are you doing up so late? You should be asleep."

"I don't wanna," Evelyn protested, "Ash's reading me stories!"

Emma turned to Ash once more, an expression of suspicion still on her face as she raised an eyebrow. "I think that's enough stories for one night, don't you think, Ash?"

Naturally, Ash didn't reply. The look on her face clearly told Emma that she was annoyed from her interference.

"Nurse Ash is going to put these books away let you get some rest." Emma stated as she picked up the scattered storybooks from Evelyn's bed, before placing them in Ash's hands. "And then, I'm going to have a little chat with her."

With the books in hand, Ash looked at Emma with an annoyed face. "Would you like me to tuck you in, Ev?" she asked, to which Evelyn agreed. After tucking her in, Emma dragged Ash out of the ward.

"What on earth are you doing?!" Emma exclaimed quietly; it was almost like a whispered yell. "This is so unprofessional, do her parents know what you're doing?!"

Ash looked completely unbothered. Through her eyes, she was simply looking after a small, vulnerable child. "She's a foster child. She told me her carers aren't very nice, therefore I'm looking after her. Is there something wrong with me looking after a sick child?"

Emma stuttered her words out, unable to believe how unbothered Ash was. "Do you even know how wrong that is? You're a nurse, not her mother!"

Ash was silent, almost too silent. She seemed uncomfortable with Emma's words.

"I have no reason to be here. I'm going home, goodbye," Ash said before storming off in a tantrum. Emma didn't know how to feel about the situation. Was it something she had to keep an eye on, or was Ash really doing something harmless? Whatever the answer was, Emma felt like she'd forgotten something.

'What have I forgotten...?' she wondered, until she suddenly remembered. Checking her phone, she realised the time. 9:55 PM, she's 5 minutes behind schedule.

"Crap!" She whispered to herself as she finally rushed to the PACU.

Chapter 6
A Red Fox's prey

Saturday, January 14th, 8:30 PM.

The deafening music pouring from the pub could be heard from blocks away. The colourful, flashing lights coming from the inside only added to the headache. It was almost like a cheap nightclub; a place Emma could never imagine herself visiting, but there she was, outside the 'Red Fox pub' with her *accomplice? Co-worker? Leader?* - Ash.

Emma, for the first time in weeks, was dressed for the occasion. She wore a knee-length, navy blue dress covered by a short, creamy-white, unbuttoned cardigan and was paired with a pair of thin, tights and black, buckled shoes. Her milk-chocolate hair was neatly curled.

Ash, on the other hand, was dressed in a more casual attire, wearing light blue baggy jeans, a dark green, baggy jumper, and black trainers. She also wore a silver cross necklace around her neck.

"My God, it's so cold…" Emma muttered, shivering as the cold air bit her bare legs.

Climbing the step that led into the pub, she turned around to make sure that Ash was following. Ash, though, was still standing opposite the door, staring at the three small steps leading into the pub.

"You' coming?" Emma asked. Ash looked up at her. She looked uncertain, even possibly vulnerable. Despite that, she said nothing and followed Emma into the noisy, crowded party.

The warm air enveloping them as they entered was immediately noticeable to both Ash and Emma, but it was the nostalgia of the environment that caught Ash's attention the most. The loud music and flashing lights reminded her of her rebellious teenage years, sneaking into clubs with her friends. The old, dark, oak furniture and red and gold flowery and geometrical patterned carpet took her back to her childhood, when her mother would drag her into the local pub. She'd play around with her mother's friends' children, earning a pack of crisps or a tub of sweets as a reward for her good behaviour.

The faint whiff of alcohol in the air reminded her of herself. Her weekends, her evenings, her mornings, her *home*.

As soon as they stepped inside, they were greeted by Charlotte and another young woman. The woman had bright, fiery orange hair, which was pulled into a neat, professional but stylish bun. She wore a long, elegant red dress, which clung to her shoulders, highlighting her piercing blue eyes. Around her torso hung a white and gold sash that said 'Happy 22nd birthday'.

"Ash, I'm so glad you made it!" Charlotte exclaimed as she hugged Ash, who didn't seem comfortable with the embrace.

"You must be April," Emma said awkwardly, smiling. "Happy birthday!"

April smiled back at Emma. "That's me. Thank you very much." Her voice was as kind as her smile.

As Ash and Emma made their way to the bar, Charlotte turned to April. "I had to invite Emma, but she's honestly ruining the vibe," she started. "I wish we could just have this be about you and your birthday."

April, who was hesitant, replied, "Well, she doesn't seem all that bad. She seems quite nice, actually. I love what you've done for me, Charlotte, it just seems… A lot, you know?"

"Come on, April. You deserve the night of your life." Charlotte replied with a smile as she held April's hands with her own. "It's your birthday, so let's make sure you have an amazing time."

Another couple entered the bar, and Charlotte greeted them. "Hello, Daniel and Rosa! I'm delighted that you're here."

April smiled joyfully and added, "Ah, Doctor Sharma, thank you for coming."

Rosa, who asked to be called just 'Rosa', replied warmly, "Happy birthday!"

Over at the bar, Ash and Emma sat side by side, each lost in their own thoughts. Emma appeared to be anxious, constantly shifting in her seat as she kept a watchful eye on the entrance, looking out for Rosa's arrival.

"If you're so desperate to talk to Charlotte, go talk to her." Ash said as she stared into her phone. "You're the one that dragged me here anyway."

"Charlotte?!" Emma whispered, frustrated and disappointed. "Are you kidding me, she didn't even say hello to me! The woman hates me!"

"Really? Didn't notice." Ash muttered sarcastically. "Go make a new friend or something. Have 'fun' and 'get stuff off your chest' or whatever you said."

Emma let out a frustrated sigh, knowing that she would have to take matters into her own hands if she wanted to enjoy the party. "Okay, fine. I will." She said before jumping off her seat and storming away.

Ash was finally alone. She didn't want to come to the damn party in the first place, the least she could get was some peace and quiet. Away from the people, the noise, the chaos. Just her, the bartender and her phone.

And alcohol. A lot of alcohol sitting behind the counter. Vodka, whiskey, brandy, lager, all the drinks that send you through a portal to peace and destruction.

Ash looked into her purse. Two £10 notes, that's enough for a drink or two. *Surely just a shot, just one small drink will be fine.*

No, tomorrow is a very important day, and she can't afford to fuck up on a murder.

Just one drink... Just a sip, just—

Ash slammed her fist into the bar table in frustration, leaning her forehead into her left hand.

'I can't. If I drink, I'll black out and won't make it to work. I need to stay sober, just for today, otherwise the plan won't work.'

Ignoring her fancy for a drink, Ash continued to stare into her phone, zoning out while she scrolled through Facebook. Sure, it wasn't interesting at all, neither did Ash care about anybody else's business, but it was better than talking to a bunch of nobodies.

Suddenly, a tall, blonde man sat down next to her. He was well-dressed, with black and white stripy shirt and beige trousers. He looked around the same age as Ash.

"Is this seat taken?" he asked, gesturing to the empty stool next to her.

Ash looked up from her phone with a start, surprised to see the man sitting next to her. She shrugged, "Go ahead," she said, not particularly interested in making conversation.

The man smiled and sat down, ordering a drink from the bartender. He turned to Ash and said, "I couldn't help but notice you over here all by yourself. Thought I'd come over and keep you company."

There was a look of confusion on Ash's face. She didn't know what to say or how to react, so she muttered "Okay," before staring back down at her phone.

"I'm Ethan." The man said. "Ethan Brown. You?"

"Ash Thomas."

Despite Ash's dry answers, clearly indicating that she doesn't want to talk, Ethan continued to try and spark a conversation.

"So, how'd you know April?" he asked.

"I uhm, I don't really know her. Her friend invited me, then my co-worker dragged me here."

"Really?" Ethan chuckled. "I don't know her that much either, we used to be neighbours until she moved out for uni. Still close friends with her parents, though, so they invited me."

Ash wasn't at all interested in the man's backstory.

"So, can I buy you a drink?" Ethan asked.

'For god sakes...' Ash thought. How could she ever say 'no' to a free drink?

I can't. Just say no.

"No, thanks." Ash replied.

"Aw, why not? It's on me, honestly."

Ash sighed. "I have work tomorrow, if I drink, I'll get hungover and miss work n' all."

"Hey, I didn't say to get totally smashed. I'm offering you one drink, that's all."

The problem is, Ash wouldn't stop at one drink, she'd buy another one, then another one, and another one until she'd collapse on the floor and spend the next day tired and hungover.

"Come on, it's a Saturday night and you're being offered a free drink. Let yourself go, have some fun. It's on me."

'Fuck it, one free drink will be fine.'

Ash caved with a huff. "Fine. A Margarita."

Ethan smirked before ordering the drink from the bartender.

Emma wandered around the bar, searching for someone she knew, someone to talk to so she didn't look like a lost duckling in a crowd of people. Staring around the dance floor, she noticed Rosa dancing with Daniel, their arms wrapped around each other in a romantic embrace as they danced to 'Brown Eyed Girl.'

Rosa looked amazing, the way her skin glimmered in the colourful lights, how her purple dress perfectly fit her body, she was just perfect. A sight so beautiful but ruined by the man who danced with her. But, tomorrow, that won't be a problem.

Emma decided to walk away and leave the couple be, continuing her search for someone she recognised. Unfortunately, the only person she knew was Charlotte. She knew if she went over there, Charlotte would just pester and humiliate her.

On the other hand, she was with April. Maybe she would act differently around her, perhaps she would be kinder. She had nothing better to do, so she approached the two young women.

"Hey." Emma spoke.

"Hi, Emma. Can we help you? Where's Ash?" Charlotte asked.

"She's sitting at the bar on her phone, being her usual introverted self." Emma joked. "I'd rather not sit silently awkward with her, so I came here."

"Well, we're a bit busy at the moment." Charlotte declared.

"Actually, I think it would be nice to get to know each other." April started. "I'm April Richardson. You already know Charlotte, what about you?"

Emma introduced herself properly to April and the three spoke for a while. For the first time, Charlotte was somewhat kind to Emma. Although, she couldn't get rid of the feeling in her stomach that Charlotte did not want Emma there. April, on the other hand, seemed very interested in Emma, so she stayed and continued to talk.

Soon after, there was a tap on Emma's back followed by a voice saying "Emmaaaa~"

She turned around to see Rosa, this time, without Daniel.

"Hi, Rose! You look incredible." Emma said happily, going in to hug Rosa.

"Aw, thanks! I had no idea you were here. You're looking amazing, too." Rosa replied, hugging Emma back.

Emma's face lit up as she heard 'I don't feel like dancing', one of her favourite songs, starting to play.

Rosa held out a hand. "Care to dance, and sing our hearts out?"

Emma took Rosa's hand as they ran to the dance floor and enjoyed the next few songs, doing ridiculously funny dance moves and singing their hearts out. As a quiet person, Emma would never dream of doing such a thing. But it didn't matter, she was with Rosa, and all she wanted was to enjoy her night with her.

Ash and Ethan had already finished several rounds of drinks and were now well into their conversation. Ash's one martini turned into two gin and tonics, and their friendly introduction had quickly turned personal as they shared stories from their lives. They soon discovered that they had a few things in common, such as attending the same comprehensive school and enjoying a social drink.

Ash stepped away for a moment, disappearing into the crowd as she went to use the restroom. As she scanned the room, she spotted Daniel deep in conversation with an unfamiliar girl, clearly obvious to Rosa's absence. The younger woman was leaning against the wall with Daniel leaning besides her, a flirtatious smirk as they spoke. Although, that was none of Ash's business, so she ignored it and continued into the restroom.

Ash had already consumed a fair amount of alcohol, and the effects were starting to set in. Her vision was slightly distorted, and she felt a slight throbbing inside her head. The dizziness made her feel unsteady on her feet, but it was nothing out of the ordinary for her. She was a seasoned drinker and had experienced this sensation many times before.

As she washed her hands in front of the mirror, Ash took a moment to reflect on her actions. The realization that she was drinking with a total stranger, someone she'd just met, left her feeling uncertain. It wasn't the alcohol that made her uneasy, but rather the realization of how out of character it was for her to be this social. It had been so long since Ash had enjoyed the company of others that the feeling was almost alien. She couldn't help but craving another drink, to feel that small yet strange rush of excitement again.

As Ash returned to the bar, Ethan offered her another drink. He handed her a small, orange, cloudy glass bottle and said, "I know you said no more alcohol, so I brought you a j2o instead."

Ash looked into the bottle, noticing how the juice fizzled up at the top. However, her mind was a blur, so she completely ignored it and took a few sips.

As time passed, Ash's symptoms started to worsen. The headache intensified and she felt increasingly nauseous. The room started to spin, making her struggle to keep her balance. She felt like vomiting at any second.

"I think... I'm... going to stand... outside... for a bit." Ash murmured, wincing at the pounding headache she felt. She rose from her seat, still clutching the juice bottle, and stumbled towards the back entrance.

"Here, let me come with you." Ethan said as he followed Ash.

"Should I get you some water, Ash? It might help yo—" Ethan suggested, but he was rudely cut off by Ash's mumbles.

"No, I'm... I'm fine, I'll be fine. Just give me 5 minutes."

Ash couldn't help but wonder what was causing her to feel this way. She wasn't a light drinker by any means and had experienced similar situations before without having such severe symptoms.

"You know, I really don't think you should be alone tonight." Ethan said as he placed his hands around Ash's waist. "How about you come home with me, and I'll look after you? I promise to take good care of you."

Ash couldn't process her own thoughts, yet alone someone else's words. She could hear Ethan speaking, but the words sounded like a foreign language, like nothing she had heard before.

She suddenly felt a push, as if someone was forcing her to move. "Come on, I'll keep you safe."

Hearing those words mixed with sudden push made Ash realize something was wrong. All the odd details from the night, such as the sizzling bubbles in her drink despite it being flat, its cloudy appearance and strange taste, and her own unusual reactions, came together in a sudden realization.

"Hold on..." Ash spoke as she gripped onto Ethan's arm, trying to keep herself stable. "Did you... Did you fucking spike me...?"

Ethan's voice sounded completely fake as he spoke. "No, of course not, what do you mean? Are you okay?"

As Ash reflected on the events of the night, a simmering anger began to rise within her, fuelled by feelings of betrayal and vulnerability. She couldn't shake the sense of disappointment in herself for daring to believe that someone might genuinely care, might truly want to understand her. But it was all a facade, a cruel deception that left her feeling foolish and exposed. The realization that he had lied, that he had betrayed her trust, ignited a raging fire within Ash, intensifying her fury with each passing moment.

"You... son of a... bitch..." She growled. "You lied to me, you asshole! You're trying to take me home and use me for your pleasure, before chucking me out onto the streets..."

"I—"

Ash refused to allow Ethan to utter another word. "How fucking dare you?!" she thundered, her arm wielding the half-empty glass bottle, which swung fiercely across his head. The bottle shattered upon impact, leaving a trail of countless cuts etched into his skin. Ethan crumpled to the floor, unconscious but mercifully alive. Ash glared at him with seething anger before flinging the remaining top half of the bottle in his direction.

The four women – April, Charlotte, Rosa, and Emma, were all drained and exhausted after a night of spirited dancing. Despite their fatigue, a strong bond had formed among them, though Charlotte and Emma remained somewhat distant, maintaining a civil but distant rapport.

"I haven't had that much fun in a long time." Rosa said joyfully.

"Neither have I, and you made it ten times better, Rose." Emma chimed in.

"I'm knackered, anyone fancy a drink?" April suggested, to which they all agreed. However, before they could make their way over to the bar, Emma noticed Ash stumbling towards them.

"Ash…?" Emma asked in concern. Ash looked like she had one too many drinks. "Are you alright? What happened—"

Before Ash could respond, she collapsed to the floor, leaving the three women behind Emma in shock.

"Oh crap, is she okay?!" Rosa exclaimed, joining Emma as they knelt beside Ash.

"She's probably had too much to drink," Emma reassured, attempting to lift Ash. "For goodness' sake, Ash…"

"I'll give you both a lift home, we can't leave her here like this." Rosa offered.

"Thank you so much, I'll keep her at mine so I can look after her." Emma replied gratefully.

After a short drive and considerable effort, Rosa dropped the pair off at Emma's house, where Ash spent the night sleeping on the sofa under Emma's watchful eye.

11:30 PM

After dropping Emma and Ash at Emma's house, Rosa and Daniel arrived back at his house where Rosa had been staying. As she walked through the door, she was greeted by Daniel's dog, Milo, who jumped up at her excitedly.

"Hello, Milo." Rosa greeted with a warm smile, gently petting the brown cockapoo.

Daniel took their coats and hung them up while Rosa expressed her concern about Emma and Ash. "I hope Emma's managing alright with Ash, she was looking pretty rough."

Daniel wrapped his arms around Rosa from behind, offering reassurance. "I'm sure she'll be fine. No need to worry. You should get yourself settled into bed. I'll join you after I feed Milo."

While Daniel headed into the kitchen, Rosa sank onto the sofa, noticing Daniel's phone resting nearby, constantly lighting up with notifications. *'Who could be messaging him this late at night...?'* Rosa wondered.

She was curious. If it were just one or two pings, she wouldn't have cared, but it pinged the entire way home. Every time Rosa asked, Daniel would reply saying it's his parents or emails.

Picking up the phone, she found it locked but glimpsed a recent message on the lock screen from an unknown number:

"I had a lot of fun tonight. I hope to see you again soon xx ;)"

Rosa's heart sank as she read the message. Just then, Daniel returned to the room and caught a sight of her on his phone.

"Who's this?" Rosa questioned, showing him the message.

Daniel remained remarkably composed, explaining, "Oh, that's just April. We got along pretty well and decided to trade numbers for work purposes."

"Work purposes? What about the winky face?!"

"Calm down, baby." Daniel urged. "It's probably just a typo. You've done the same typo before, remember?" Daniel said, reminding Rosa of the time she messaged an old boss and wrote a winking face instead of a happy face. The calmness in his voice and body was reassuring, there was nothing hinting of any suspicion, so Rosa dismissed her previous thoughts.

The two, and Milo, all headed to bed. As the other two drifted off to sleep, Rosa couldn't ignore the strange feeling that Daniel might have been lying. She doesn't believe that Daniel would ever lie to her, but what if he did? What if she'd have to go through the feeling of breakup *again*?

'He's not lying.' Rosa reassured herself. The way Daniel treats her like a princess and loves her like a wife, there's no way he'd lie to her. Besides, Daniel isn't the type of guy who'd do such a thing. Rosa knew deep down that she'd found her other side, her lover, and they'll spend the rest of their lives together.

Rosa finally decided that there wasn't enough proof of anything, so she discarded her thoughts and fell asleep peacefully, with Daniel by her side and Milo sleeping between them.

Chapter 7
I am bad. Bad is me.

Sunday, January 15th, 7:18 AM.

Emma stood in her kitchen, the soft murmur of the radio providing a gentle backdrop as she bused herself preparing breakfast and lunch. Despite feeling weary from the previous night, she couldn't shake off the embarrassment of Ash's reaction. Still, she refused to let that overshadow the enjoyable moments shared with Rosa and her newfound acquaintance, April. Even Charlotte had surprised her with a rare display of kindness.

She walked into the living room when she heard a yawn.

"Finally awake, huh?" She asked.

Ash, who had just woken up, was visually very confused. She looked around the room and rubbed her eyes, trying to recognize where she was.

"You're at my house, Ash. Do you remember anything that happened last night?"

Ash remained silent. She couldn't remember anything; she didn't even know what was going on. Why was she at Emma's house? Was she really there, or was she dreaming?

Emma passed a bowl of cereal and a glass of water to Ash. "Eat up. I wouldn't be surprised if you were dehydrated from the amount of alcohol you drank last night."

As Ash slowly regained her bearings, fragments of memory began to resurface. The mention of a bar triggered a name in her mind: Ethan.

"Ethan?" Emma echoed, puzzled by the unfamiliar name.

Ash struggled to articulate her thoughts, but the pieces started to fit together. "He spiked me..."

Emma's expression shifted to one of disbelief. "Spiked you? What happened exactly?"

Unable to recall the entire sequence of events, Ash recounted her fragmented memories from the night before, stopping short at a blurry point in their encounter. "And the rest is a blur…"

Emma was at a loss for words. "I had no idea, Ash. I'm so sorry."

"It's fine," Ash replied, finishing the bowl of cereal and water.

"Hey, Ash. Today's the uh… cyanide poisoning day, right?" Emma's voice trembled slightly as she broached the topic, a sickening feeling knotting her stomach. A part of her questioned the morality of their actions, even as she followed Ash's lead.

"Shit, yeah. I totally forgot." Ash muttered; her thoughts momentarily distracted.

"Our shifts start at half 8. Quickly go home and change, don't forget anything. I'll see you at the hospital." Emma instructed.

As Ash made her way home, she wrestled with memories of Ethan and the uncertainty surrounding his fate. Had he escaped? Had she unwittingly caused harm? The answers remained elusive, leaving Ash grappling with unanswered questions and a lingering sense of unease.

8:15 AM

Emma sat anxiously in the staffroom, her eyes darting to the clock as she waited for Ash to arrive.

'She better not be late…' she thought. Rosa and Daniel hadn't shown up yet either. It was only her in the room, apart from Anderson who was in his office next door. That was nothing to worry about, though, as Anderson had been keeping to himself ever since Kat's passing, his

presence confined to the solitude of his office. His withdrawal was palpable, leaving a sense of mystery surrounding him. Nobody dared to intrude on whatever grief or contemplation he was immersed in, except perhaps his confidant David.

So far, everything was going smoothly. The lone security camera in the room hadn't undergone an upgrade yet. Anderson had mentioned it would be the last one to be updated since it was situated in the staffroom. Emma had already positioned the new tub of coffee beans beside the old, nearly depleted one. It contained just enough beans for a single cup. That was the one Ash would poison.

It was a very risky plan; everything had to be entirely perfect. Even one little flaw would result in the wrong person being poisoned. Or, the whole lot of staff would've been poisoned, except for Emma, Ash, and any other staff who don't drink coffee.

Fortunately, if Ash was the best at something, it would be predicting what was going to happen. Though she was only a nurse, not many knew what a genius she could be, especially with her knowledge of murder. When she sets her sights on someone, she will study every single thing about that person, from their habits to their routine, their secrets and everything in between. Ash knows her targets better than anybody else in the world.

Ash walked in abruptly, making a beeline for the coffee. She sneaked the cyanide into the beans, snapped the lid shut, and backed away before anyone else showed up.

"Feeling alright now?" Emma inquired from her seat, sticking to their promise not to talk about the cyanide while in the hospital.

Ash responded, "Yeah, thanks for looking after me earlier. I'd probably be blacked out if I was at my house."

Rosa and Daniel then arrived.

"Hey, Rose!" Emma said excitedly.

"Morning, Gem! How are you feeling this morning, Ash?" Rosa asked with concern.

"I'm alright now, thanks to Emma." Ash said, acting as if it were a normal day.

"That's my Gem. Always looking after others, aren't you." Rosa smiled, sitting down next to Emma.

"I'm beat after last night. Anyone want a coffee?" Daniel offered. Emma's heart sank in her chest. Their plan was coming to life right in front of her eyes, and there was no turning back.

Luckily, no one took Daniel up on the offer. Rosa brought her own coffee in a flask which she had prepared earlier.

A few moments later, the sound of the boiling kettle dominated the room, filling Emma's ears. She could hear it over the muffled conversations of the other staff that entered the room, over the sound of footsteps, over the sound of Rosa talking…

'Shit, Rosa's talking to me.' Emma thought, before snapping out of her little zoned out world.

"Gem? Are you okay?" Rosa asked.

"Yeah, I'm alright, I just zoned out… Last night was tiring, I didn't get much sleep."

"Neither did I." Rosa laughed. "Should we head over to the Emergency department? I'm sure there's already patients waiting for us."

Emma smiled and agreed. Rosa's laugh, her company, made Emma feel warm inside. For a moment, she almost forgot about the tragic events which were about to happen. Shortly after, the two left the room.

'Emma doesn't know what she's missing.' Ash mused silently as her gaze lingered on Daniel, who savoured his coffee from across the room. A sense of satisfaction washed over her at the flawless execution of her plan, every detail perfectly falling into place. What she found more interesting, though, were the few steps she had woven into the plan, like carefully placed brushstrokes on a masterpiece.

She had some leftover cyanide after pouring most of it into the first batch of coffee beans, so she decided to empty the remaining amount into the fresh jar. Not enough to be lethal, but enough to get sick. It was undoubtedly a risky move, but if it provides entertainment to her, she's happy. If it added an extra layer of excitement to her little game, it's definitely worth the gamble.

As the clock struck 8:30 AM, signalling the start of Ash's shift, she reluctantly tore her gaze from Daniel. Regrettably, she wouldn't be able to witness the gradual decline of his health, but such sacrifices were inevitable. With a resigned sigh, she set off to begin her duties, wherever she was needed first.

As Daniel sipped his morning coffee, unaware of the deadly concoction lurking within, a sense of routine enveloped him. The bitter taste of the brew mingled with the anticipation of another day at work. Little did he know, with each sip, he was sealing his fate.

The restroom beckoned, a brief interlude before the grind of his daily responsibilities. But as Daniel stood up, a sudden wave of unease washed over him, a premonition of the impending horror. The first tendrils of cyanide began their insidious dance through his bloodstream.

Initially imperceptible, the poison worked its way through Daniel's body with ruthless efficiency. His heart, once steady and strong, now hammered against his ribs like a prisoner desperate for escape. A vice tightened around his chest, constricting his breath until each inhale felt like drawing air through a straw. Vertigo set in, the world spinning in a disorientating blur as if reality itself had tilted off its axis.

Confusion fogged his mind, thick and suffocating, as though he were trapped in a nightmare from which he couldn't wake from. His legs betrayed him, buckling beneath the weight of his faltering body. Darkness encroached upon his vision, a swarm of black dots devouring the light all that remained was darkness.

With a final, futile struggle, Daniel collapsed to the floor, his body limp and lifeless, a mere puppet cut loose from its strings. Hours stretched into eternity as he lay motionless, the poison claiming its victory in the stillness of the restroom, a silent witness to his untimely demise.

It didn't take long for Rosa and Emma's first patient of the day to arrive. Gareth, an elderly man in his 80s, was brought in by ambulance following his first seizure. Emma stood by his side, checking his vital signs and performing quick examinations. As they waited for the MRI results, Rosa addressed their patient with a tone that radiated compassion and empathy.

"It'll be around 15 minutes to an hour before we get those results," Rosa started. "In the meantime, we're going to need to keep an eye on you and make sure you're stable and comfortable." She said, with compassion and empathy in her voice, that made it clear she truly cared about her patients.

Gareth nodded with a smile. "You two are angels. Thank you for being here."

The kind comment made both nurses smile, and Emma replied, "We're glad to be help you feel better."

"You do God's work," the man said. "Without you doctors and nurses, I wouldn't have been able to experience the amazing things I've been able to do."

"It's a pleasure." Rosa said. "What amazing things have you done in your life?"

"In my younger days, I used to spend my time smoking with friends, getting into all sorts of trouble. It was innocent fun back then," he began, a nostalgic gleam in his eyes. "Then, along came my darling wife, Vanessa. We had kids, who've grown up to make me incredibly proud. However, life threw a curveball at me when, at the age of 40, I was diagnosed with bowel cancer."

Gareth continued to talk about his 5-year-long recovery, mentioning his passion for poetry, and how he eventually become one of the top poets in the country. "Since my diagnosis, I've had the privilege of witnessing my children and grandchildren grow into adults. Life, my friend, is a true blessing, and you won't fully comprehend that until you've become old and rusty like me," he reflected, a hint of wisdom in his voice.

Pausing to catch his breath, he continued, addressing the younger generation directly. "You youngsters should savour every moment, for life is a fleeting thing. Every second wasted is a second you'll never retrieve. When you're young, you tend to take it all for granted. One day, you blink, and suddenly you're lying in a hospital bed. Your wife has passed, your children are grown, and the end is near. So, make your mark on this earth, live your life to the fullest. Don't dwell on the past or worry excessively about the future. Today is your day to live, and tomorrow is a day that will arrive soon enough. You never know when your time will come, so make the most of what you've been given and leave your mark upon the world."

Rosa and Emma sat in stunned silence as the man concluded his poignant speech. Their expressions spoke volumes, mirroring their deep contemplation of his words.

"That was... incredibly poetic. Very eye-opening." Emma firmly said, her voice tingled with awe.

The man chuckled. "I told you, I'm a poet. We poets see life in a way no ordinary person sees it, and we use our words to show you the beauty of the world, the beauty of living."

Rosa and Emma were moved by the elderly man's words, reflecting on their own lives and experiences. They realized that every moment was precious and worth savouring, every day a chance to leave a mark on the world. The man's words and his experiences served as a reminder for Rosa and Emma to cherish each day and make the most of every opportunity.

A short while later, the MRI results returned, and Rosa transferred him to an epilepsy specialist for additional tests. The second the man left the room, Emma wrapped her arms around Rosa.

Rosa was taken aback by the sudden embrace, but she found comfort in the warmth of Emma's hug. "Hugging me?" she questioned softly, a hint of surprise in her voice.

"Thank you for being here." Emma murmured, still enveloping Rosa. "Everything he said was completely true, I just want you to know how grateful I am for you."

Rosa's heart swelled with emotions as she returned the embrace, feeling a profound sense of gratitude in their bond. "You're welcome. I wouldn't be the person I am today without you."

After a moment of shared understanding, the two women reluctantly pulled away, though the connection between them lingered.

"I suppose we should get going with our next case…" Emma smiled softly, her face flustered from their hug.

And so, with renewed resolve and a strengthened bond, the two women continued on with their duties, ready to face whatever challenges lay ahead.

12:30

After four long hours, Emma was finally granted her lunch break. In the staffroom, Ash awaited her arrival.

"How's your shift going?" Emma asked, reaching into her bag for the lunch she had prepared earlier.

"Not great." Ash sighed, rising from her seat and motioning for Emma to follow. "Come on."

Confused, Emma trailed behind Ash as they ascended to the roof. Seated side by side, they both felt the chill of the winter breeze.

"Isn't it a bit cold to be sitting out here?" Emma asked. They gazed out at the busy carpark below and the swathes of green space.

"I like the numb feeling," Ash remarked, her eyes fixed on the ground. "It makes me feel something intense instead of the guilt that follows me."

"Ah, right." Emma acknowledged, unwrapping her lunch. "Want a sandwich?"

"No thanks."

Emma quietly nibbled on her sandwich, Ash remained beside her in contemplation.

"Emma." Ash began, her gaze still fixed on the ground.

Emma turned to Ash; her mouth filled with sandwich. "Yeah?"

"Why does bad follow me everywhere?"

Emma swallowed a bite and sighed before responding, "It doesn't. It's you."

"But it does."

Emma felt the urge to ask about Ash's life. It had always been a mystery to everyone at the hospital, nobody really knows what happened before Ellie got sick. However, she knew that if she asked, Ash would get annoyed and wouldn't answer a single question, so the best option is to let nature take its course and allow Ash to open up on her own terms.

"A year changes a lot, you know." Ash began. "I haven't always been this monster. I was once a normal woman. I had a life, a family, a home. But all of that was taken away from me. Now I am no longer a mother, a wife, or a human being, but a shadow of my former self."

Emma was shocked to hear Ash speak so candidly, but she remained composed and silent. Although Ash's silence prompted Emma to inquire further.

"What happened?"

"How much do you want to know?"

"All of it."

Ash opened up about her past, revealing fragments about her difficult childhood. "Being a kid was hard," she began. "My mother was an alcoholic, and I never knew what happened to my father or grandparents. It was just me and my mother against the world."

In her early adulthood, Ash found solace in Charlie, her ex-husband. "We were happy," she recalled. "We started a family. I had my first child, Arthur. He would've been 8 now, but just like Ellie, I failed to keep him alive. He was stillborn, I was devastated. Doctors told me I'd never be able to have kids."

Determined, Ash and Charlie continued to try for another child, facing countless disappointments until Ellie came into their lives. "When Ellie was born," Ash paused, her voice wavering, "I discovered that Charlie was having an affair. We divorced soon after."

The challenges didn't end there. "Then, my mother died of leukaemia," Ash continued. "Since then, it's just been me and Ellie against the world. Despite my troubled past, we tried to live a normal life. I didn't bother with relationships, I just wanted Ellie to be happy."

Tragedy struck when Ellie fell seriously ill. "I was foolish," Ash admitted. "I brushed off her symptoms as a cold until they become unbearable. Rushing her to the A&E, she fell into a coma and spent three agonizing weeks there. I prayed relentlessly for her recovery, clinging to hope with every fibre of my being."

The narrative paused, leaving Emma to grasp the weight of Ash's struggles. "And, well, you know the rest from there," Ash concluded, her voice heavy with emotion."

"What was life like without Ellie?" Emma inquired softly.

"It was sickening," Ash replied. "I did nothing. I lost two stone in a month, couldn't eat or drink for weeks." Ash continued to talk about how she turned to alcohol. "Safe to say it saved me from dying of starvation. Things never got easier, but I did find distractions. Most of which were plans to get my revenge."

"There's support available, though. Why didn't you look for help?" Emma pressed gently.

"I didn't want it," Ash admitted bitterly. "There was no point. No amount of help would give me my daughter back. All I wanted was revenge, then the sweet experience of suicide. But the day I killed Quinn was the day I discovered my new joy. My reason to live. It made me strong and powerful, all the things I've never been before. I become a heartless monster."

Emma fell into silence, rendered speechless by Ash's words.

"Sometimes it's good to be bad. It makes you feel alive again, gives you a sense of purpose. I may not be a good person, but at least I'm enjoying myself."

"You know, things do get better." Emma argued peacefully. "You don't have to be the bad guy."

"Some crimes are beyond forgiveness, and some souls cannot be saved. I am a lost cause. Nothing will turn me back into the person I used to be."

Emma sighed deeply, gathering her thoughts. "I've been through stuff as well, Ash. I lost my sister two years ago. She was my best friend; we were like two peas in a pod. Her death was sudden. It destroyed both me and my family. Eventually, we began to see the good side of life again. We escaped the darkness."

"And I'm still trapped here. Glued, taped, buried, there's no getting out. This is who I am, Emma. I'm a product of destruction. No amount of your glue, tape or plasters can put me back together. Some are drawn to the darkness; others flee from it. Some escape, others don't, but in the end, it claims us all."

Emma lowered her gaze, feeling defeated. She had nothing to say, it was like she was arguing with a parrot, Ash always had the last word, and every damn time it was something she couldn't compete with.

"Our break is almost over." Ash declared, rising to her feet. "Let's go."

As Emma returned to the emergency department, she scanned the area for Rosa but couldn't find her.

'*Maybe she's still on break*', Emma thought, but her assumption waned after ten minutes passed with no sign of Rosa. It was unusual for Rosa to be late, let alone a whole ten minutes. She was always punctual, often arriving early.

Moments later, Emma spotted Rosa walking down the hallway, her expression wrought with heartbreak.

'*Shit*'. Emma cursed inwardly as dread gnawed at her stomach with each step Rosa took.

"Are you okay? What happened?" Emma asked, her concern evident, though she already knew the answer. Rosa didn't respond; instead, she collapsed into Emma's arms, sobbing into her shoulder. Her words were muffled and incomprehensible amidst her tears. Feeling Rosa's anguish only intensified Emma's guilt; she knew she was the cause of Rosa's pain.

"Rose…" Emma murmured softly, wrapping her arms around Rosa.

Tears welled up in Emma's own eyes. "It's okay, tell me what happened…"

Rosa attempted to compose herself, wiping away her tears before whispering, "I was… called… To a code blue… It was Dan…"

Rosa couldn't bring herself to finish Dan's name before succumbing to another bout of tears.

"I'm so sorry…" Emma whispered, holding Rosa tightly as she wept.

"I… I'm going to go home…" Rosa managed through her sobs.

"That's a good idea. Should I come with you?" Emma offered.

"Thanks, Gem, but I… I want to be alone for a bit…" Rosa replied, her voice strained with emotion.

As Rosa left the scene, Emma was left astonished. She had never seen Rosa in such distress, and knowing it was all her fault made things feel a million times worse. What made matters worse, though, was knowing she had to hide these emotions for the rest of the day. If anyone asked what was wrong, she would have no explanation. Rosa's the one who had lost a loved one, not her.

Anderson sat facing the wall, appearing as though he was staring at the plain, blue-painted surface. In reality, his gaze was lost in space, oblivious to the knocking at the door until the unexpected guest entered, jolting him back to the present moment.

Spinning his chair around, Anderson greeted David, who had just walked in. "Ah, David! Lovely to see you, come in."

Anderson noticed the uncertainty in David's voice as he spoke. "Good evening, Joel. There's been another… Incident."

Anderson paused when he heard David say this. He prayed that this incident wasn't something related to the past few days, but somehow, he knew this wouldn't be good.

"There's been another murder." David declared.

Anderson sighed. "*Another* murder? Are you sure it's definitely a murder?"

"It was a murder, Joel. And if my theory is correct, so was the lab incident." David explained, his tone grave. "Doctor Daniel Graham was discovered at quarter past nine by Doctor Oakley Whitlock. He was pronounced dead at the scene. My team are currently conducting on an autopsy, but preliminary findings suggest cyanide poisoning."

The gravity of the situation weighed heavily on Anderson. Multiple murders in such a short span of time felt surreal. He knew it meant confronting significant challenges, ones he wished to avoid.

"I advise that you call the police for further investigation. Do we have any updates on the detectives?" David inquired.

"None. I haven't heard from the police or the detectives."

"Those god damn cops are useless." David muttered.

"They're in the same situation as us, Neil. Not enough staff, too much work."

"But this is a murder case." David stated firmly. "Four murders in the last week or two, Joel, do you know how serious this is? There is a murderer in this hospital, and the later we find them, the more lives it's going to cost. You can't keep sitting there and wait for a miracle to happen."

"You're right." Anderson nodded, before grabbing a sticky note pad and clicking his pen. "Who was it that you said discovered the body?"

The two began to note their suspicions and start a plan on how they'd catch the murderer. The police arrived soon after and began their own investigation. Rumours about the murder spree quietly spread through the hospital walls, with each person sharing their own theories and lies to the rumour.

Chapter 8
It's just a bad day.

Monday, January 16th, 8:00 AM.

The morning had already been a rough one for Emma. She overslept because her phone died overnight, rendering her alarm useless. Then, she discovered she had left the fridge door open all night. The idea of spending the day with Ash only heightened her stress. To make matters worse, Emma hadn't slept until 4 AM; she had spent the entire night worrying about Rosa, who hadn't responded to any of her messages or calls.

A sinking feeling gnawed at Emma's gut, foretelling that today would be another challenging day. With a string of recent difficulties and the day starting on such a sour note, she felt little optimism. Despite her complaints, as the clock struck 8, it was time to leave.

As usual, Emma headed to the staffroom before the start of her shift. It buzzed with activity, particularly because the medical students were present. However, today felt quite different. Conversations were hushed, creating an eerie atmosphere. The absence of Rosa, who Emma had never worked without, added to the unease. Scanning the room, she couldn't find Ash, but spotted April and Charlotte chatting in a corner.

Approaching them with a smile, Emma initiated small talk. "Hey, guys! How are you?"

After exchanging pleasantries, Emma noted the peculiar atmosphere. "What's going on? Something feels… off."

Although Emma suspected it was related to Daniel, she was curious about the rumours circulating.

"The police have been investigating the hospital," April replied.

Quickly interjecting, Charlotte added with an excited tone, "Rumours say there was a murder. Some even say there were two."

"It's unsettling, isn't it?" April remarked. "To think an innocent life was taken away so suddenly, especially here at the hospital…"

"There are some sick bastards out there," Charlotte chimed in.

Emma's mood shifted as regret and guilt washed over her once more. However, her attention was diverted when Charlotte exclaimed, "Ash!"

Turning around, Emma saw Ash standing behind her, startling her with her sudden appearance.

"Good morning, guys. Ready for another stressful day?" Ash joked, though her tone lacked warmth.

Charlotte replied excitedly to Ash's question. They were working together for most of the day, something Charlotte's been looking forward to for ages. Soon after, the two medical students left for a quick meeting before their shifts.

Turning to Ash, Emma mentioned the topic from the previous day. "So, I was thinking about yesterday. You've been through a lot, so I thought maybe we could go out one day, perhaps to the beach or a café." Emma continued to explain that a day out would be good for Ash to relax, but as she spoke, she noticed Ash's face change ever so slightly. The same face that leads to something Emma didn't want to hear.

"You've got the wrong idea, Emma." Ash stated, almost like a warning. "Me and you are not *friends*. You're nothing more than a tool, and I don't need you for anything other than my game."

Emma felt a mix of embarrassment, anger and shame. She thought they had built some sort of connection, that maybe, just *maybe* she could help Ash become a better person. However, Ash's words extinguished that hope, leaving Emma feeling furious.

"I am not a tool," Emma asserted. "I'm not your helper, I'm not your toy, I'm not—"

"Yes, you are," Ash interrupted, her tone chilling, reminiscent of the day Kat died. "You're my tool, and you do as I say. Try and disobey me, just try it, and you'll fucking regret it."

Ash's threat put Emma back in her place, back where she was when she started. Scared. Vulnerable. *Weak*. She looked around the room, hoping that someone else spotted her in this uncomfortable situation. Maybe someone would come save her, but nobody did. She was trapped *again*.

"Before I go, I have a favour to ask," Ash said. "Sharp items interest me. Get me a scalpel."

"A scalpel? How the hell—"

"You know exactly where to get a scalpel," Ash said. "Get me one, it's not that hard. I want it by one PM, got it?"

With a quiver in her voice, Emma replied, "okay," before the pair separated to start their jobs.

8:45 AM.

"I'm so excited for today, where are we going first?!" Charlotte asked cheerfully as she walked down the hallway with Ash.

"Doctor Whitlock has ordered blood tests for a patient in room 204," Ash said. "Ever done a blood test before?"

"I've practiced a few times on arm models, this will be my first time on a real patient though." Charlotte replied.

Arriving at the room, Ash knocked the door and entered, greeted by a family. A man in his late thirties stood alongside two children—a daughter, approximately nine years old, and a son around seven. In the bed lay a woman, also in her late thirties.

Great. Ash thought. A family, one of the things she hated seeing the most.

Ash introduced herself and Charlotte kindly to the family.

"Darling, do you mind keeping the kids outside for a short while?" The woman asked her husband.

"Of course." The man said. "Millie, Logan, enough messing around, let's wait outside while mummy gets some medicine."

"They don't have to leave," Ash interjected with a polite smile. "They're welcome to stay, I don't mind."

"It's okay, a bit of peace and quiet would be nice." The woman, Kathrine, joked. "That's Millie and Logan, my children. I love them dearly, but you know how annoying children can be sometimes."

Ash forced a chuckle, feeling irritated by Kathrine's remarks. People who are ungrateful for their children should be punished, Ash thought, and she was the perfect example. *Some people don't deserve kids.*

Ash and Charlotte began to prepare for the blood test, with Ash quickly explaining the procedure before asking Kathrine's consent to do the test. Once she had given the go-ahead, they began.

"Remember, Charlotte, 45-degree angle." Ash reminded her as Charlotte prepared the needle. However, as she struck the needle into the patient, Kathrine groaned, and a small stream of blood fell down her arm instead of into the tube. Realizing she had made a mistake, Charlotte began to panic.

"Ah, I'm so sorry!" she said, trying to hide her nerves, but as she moved to adjust the needle, she accidentally caused Kathrine more pain.

"Its... okay...!" Kathrine said hesitantly. Ash, seeing Charlotte's nervous state, quickly took over to remove the needle from the patient's arm. She then allowed Charlotte to try again, and this time, she was able to get a small amount of blood into the tube, though it wasn't enough. Ash stepped in to finish the test, and the rest of the blood samples went much more smoothly.

Charlotte watched Ash closely during the test, joining in on the small talk when she could. She felt ashamed of her mistakes, even though both Kathrine and Ash tried to reassure her.

"My daughter, Millie, really wants to be a nurse like you two." Kathrine said. "Logan, though, is obsessed with football."

These types of patients were the worst for Ash. The type of person who blabbers about their life the whole time, it's especially worse when they talk about kids.

"Ah, just like me and my brother." Charlotte replied. "He's studying law in university now, though. Something about being a lawyer..."

Kathrine looked up with thought, a smile painted on her face. "Aw, I bet your mother is so proud of you both. Seeing your children growing up is beautiful, I couldn't be prouder of my babies."

Ash finished the procedure and placed the samples away neatly, visually annoyed by Kathrine's words. She and Charlotte then left the room, where the children ran back to their mother as the husband followed.

'Why can't I have a family. Why do her kids get to live but not mine.' Ash thought.

"Hey, Ash, I'm gonna' go to the toilet quickly. I'll meet you with the next case soon." Charlotte announced before sprinting to the staff restrooms. She chose these restrooms specifically; it would be the quietest place.

Charlotte clung to the skink, gazing at her reflection in the restroom mirror. Tears welled up in the corners of her eyes, silently tracing down her cheeks.

"*Idiot.*" she murmured to herself, each repetition echoing her self-directed criticism. "*I'm an idiot, an idiot, an idiot.*"

Staring into the sink, she felt a wave of shame and embarrassment wash over her. She prided herself on not making mistakes. She *had* to be flawless in everything she did. Her parents expected nothing less from their perfect daughter. So, when she did falter, it was intolerable. It wasn't something she could brush off or forget; it was a reminder of her imperfection, a source of self-inflicted misery.

It had always been this way. In school, a B instead of an A wasn't met with praise but with disappointment. Her parents viewed it as a failure to appreciate their investment, a lack of effort in pursuit of perfection. While her relationship with her parents wasn't contentious, their high expectations weighed heavily on her, and when she fell short, she felt their disapproval keenly. Even in their absence, the habit of agonizing over mistakes persisted.

"Cmon, Charlotte." She chided herself. "Ash is waiting for you."

With that, she left the restroom, only to encounter Anderson exiting the director's office adjacent to it.

"Oh, hello. I've never seen you before, one of the medical students?" Anderson asked kindly, his gaze catching the tear stains on her cheeks. "Ah, have you been crying?"

Confused by the unexpected encounter, Charlotte responded honestly. "Yeah, um, it's nothing. I was just upset over a mistake I made."

"Hey, people make mistakes. Surely it wasn't bad enough to bring you to tears," Anderson reassured her.

"I was giving someone a blood test but failed twice…"

"A significant part of being a student is making mistakes, you know," Anderson offered comfortingly. "The important thing is learning from them. Back in medical school years ago, I once mixed up a bunch of medical documents. Nobody knows till this day…"

Charlotte chuckled at the anecdote. "Really? That's actually quite funny. Are you a doctor here?"

She was surprised when Anderson introduced himself as the hospital director. "I run this place, and even I still make mistakes today."

Charlotte would've been lying if she said Anderson didn't improve her mood. Knowing that someone as prominent as him also made mistakes made her feel better about her own slip-ups. After all, she was just a student, with years of experience ahead of her to hone her skills.

"Thanks, you cheered me up a bit." Charlotte said, offering a grateful smile. The two continued their conversation, getting along remarkably well. In fact, Charlotte completely forgot about the task she was supposed to attend to, and so did Anderson.

"You remind me a lot of someone, you know." Anderson remarked, still chuckling at their earlier exchange.

"Who would that be?"

"An old friend of mine. She was just like you, bubbly and energetic, confident." Anderson said with a smile, remembering the woman he used to know. "Her name was Kat."

10:24 AM.

After completing the task that Charlotte never turned up to, Ash decided to spend her free time with Evelyn. As she entered the paediatric ward, she wasn't surprised to find Evelyn alone. While other children were surrounded by friends and family, Evelyn lay in her bed, with only the nurses for company.

"Hey, Ev'!" Ash greeted with a friendly smile as she approached Evelyn. She quickly noticed Evelyn's deteriorating condition. Her face was paler than before, and she seemed drained of energy. To Ash's concern, Evelyn didn't even respond, prompting Ash to gently shake her.

"Evelyn?"

The young girl yawned with a stretch.

"Ah, sleepy, were you?" Ash smiled in relief. "I've got you a little toy."

Evelyn perked up at the mention of a toy. Ash retrieved a small teddy from her pocket, a pink, fluffy elephant plush.

"This is Ellie the Elephant," Ash introduced, passing the teddy to Evelyn, who hugged it tightly. "She used to belong to a very lucky little girl called Ellie."

"Ellie? But the elephant is called Ellie!" Evelyn laughed.

"I know, isn't it funny?" Ash smiled. "Ellie was my own daughter; she was just like you. You would've been best friends."

"Can I see her?" Evelyn asked. Ash hesitated, not wanting to upset Evelyn with the truth about Ellie's passing.

"Would you like to see a photo?"

Evelyn agreed, so Ash showed her a photo of Ellie on her phone. It was a picture of her playing at a park, the one just outside the hospital.

"I've been there before!" Evelyn exclaimed happily. "Can we go there?"

As much as Ash wanted to fulfil Evelyn's wish, she knew it wasn't possible given Evelyn's condition and the limited time they had.

"It's a bit cold outside, so how about we wait another day?" Ash suggested. "For now, how about we do some colouring and I'll put your hair into pigtails? Just like Ellie does in this picture."

Evelyn agreed, so she began colouring pictures of her and Ash doing all sorts of things, like days at the beach and playing in the park. One picture, though, caught Ash's attention. It was a picture of Ash sitting next to Evelyn's hospital bed, and Evelyn was sleeping.

"What's going on in that picture?" Ash asked, tying Evelyn's hair into pigtails.

"That's me," Evelyn explained, pointing to the drawing of herself. "And that's you, after I've had my surgery!"

Ash stared at the photo in confusion. "Surgery? What surgery, darling?"

"The surgery I'm having on my tummy."

'Surgery...?' The thought of Evelyn going in for surgery did not make her happy, especially after what happened to Ellie. Why didn't Ash know about this? Especially after Emma had been working with her not long before, why didn't Emma tell her?

"I didn't know you were having surgery. When is it?" Ash asked, but Evelyn didn't know. At that moment, Ash decided when the surgery would be.

It would never happen.

There are thousands of medications in the world. Surgery *cannot* be the only option.

'Are her carers so stupid to allow such a thing? Do they even know what's going to happen?' That's when Ash came to a conclusion. They don't want Evelyn to survive. They don't care about the monsters in this hospital that can take a life away faster than light speed, they don't care about the dangers they're putting their 'child' into. In fact, they're probably the reason that Evelyn is in the hospital. *'The greedy bastards are only in it for the money.'*

"What if that surgery never happened, Evelyn?" Ash asked curiously. Evelyn replied with a shrug. The young girl didn't fully understand what the surgery was, neither what it did.

"Would you prefer me to look after you?"

Evelyn smiled softly, stroking the elephant teddy. "Yes please."

Ash smiled back. "Okay. I'll keep you safe. *I promise.*"

A mother's promise is a promise that should never be broken.

This promise was a promise that would never be broken.

11:05 AM.

Patients were flying into the emergency room with injuries as small as a sprain, to problems as complicated as a stroke, and the fact Emma had a list of twelve patients to assess alone because Ash hadn't turned up made things worse. The two were supposed to be working in triage, but *someone* decided not to show up.

Emma was somewhat glad that Ash hadn't turned up, that means she wouldn't have to put up with her bullshit. On the other hand, she wasn't in the mood to be stressing over twelve strangers (and counting.)

"Where the hell is she?!" Emma muttered under her breath as she tidied up the thermometer, catching the attention of the elderly woman she was examining, who responded with a confused groan.

"Sorry, just thinking aloud." Emma apologized, addressing the elderly patient. "My colleague, should be here, but she's running late."

"Huuuuh?" The elderly woman groaned again with a knit expression. She had dementia and her caregiver had left her unsupervised, so she couldn't communicate what she was thinking or feeling beyond her confused grunts. Emma recognized the woman's condition, being experienced with dementia from her previous employment at a care home, and continued the assessment promptly.

"Sorry I'm late, lost track of time." Ash interjected brusquely as she entered the room.

Emma's eyebrows furrowed in annoyance. "Took you long enough." She then informed Ash on what she'd already completed in the assessment, but as she explained, the elderly patient had slipped off the chair, collapsing unconscious on the floor. Both nurses sprang into action, immediately assessing the patient's vital signs and responsiveness.

"Announce a code blue, triage room 4, full-code." Emma declared as she commenced CPR on the patient, her heart pounding in her chest. Resuscitation was the aspect of hospital work Emma loathed the most; lives were quite literally in her hands.

The elderly woman's caregiver rushed in upon hearing the intercom announcement, but Emma remained focused on the task at hand, ensuring each compression was timed, forceful, and accurate. Despite her efforts, when she checked for a pulse, there was none.

"I'm not giving up, not when it's my choice," Emma muttered to herself, determined to persist with CPR despite the strain. As exhaustion threatened to overwhelm her, Ash, noticing Emma's struggle, intervened and took over CPR.

As Emma caught her breath, she observed Ash's efforts to revive the patient. Something felt off about seeing Ash trying to *save* someone's life, when all she cared about was her cruel game. Her sight was disturbed when more staff rushed into the room.

"She's got a pulse," Ash announced triumphantly to the team. "Get her to the ER with an IV and fluids."

The rest of the staff quickly moved the woman onto a stretcher and wheeled her to the ER. Within seconds, the triage room had become silent, except for the sound of Emma still trying to catch her breath.

Emma couldn't comprehend what happened. Within barely five minutes, a woman almost died, and now it's gone back to silence. Just Emma and Ash. The situation itself wasn't overwhelming, but after being on edge for so long, Emma couldn't help but let her held-back tears fall from her eyes.

"What are you crying for? I'm the one that saved the damn woman." Ash said after noticing the tears.

"I'm sorry, it... it's a lot..."

"Stop crying, there's a whole waiting room of people needing to be assessed. Now's not the time."

Emma wiped away her tears. "Yeah. You're right." As she stood up, someone stood behind the blue curtain knocked the wall and entered the room. Ash's heart sunk when she saw the bright, yellow-green waistcoat. It was a police officer, and he didn't want Ash, but Emma. Luckily, no one was in trouble, they just wanted an interview about Quinn's murder, being that she was the one who found the body. As nervous as she was, she followed the officer and completed the interview while Ash worked with another nurse in triage.

11:20 AM

Anderson was sat in his office, engrossed in an important meeting, when an urgent knock abruptly shattered the atmosphere. The knocker, David, barged in without waiting for permission, a habit Anderson had grown accustomed to.

"Ah, hello, David," Anderson greeted, introducing the two police officers beside him. "This is Detective Ioan Evans, the senior law enforcement officer, and Lily Mae, one of the junior officers. Are you here to join the meeting?"

Anderson couldn't help but notice David's breathlessness, as if he had just ran a mile. "There's been an incident. A very serious one," David blurted out, his words tumbling over each other. "There's been a stabbing moments ago on the second floor, in the oncology department. The suspect is a male, wearing a grey and yellow hoodie and a facemask."

The two officers exchanged panicked glances as Detective Ioan swiftly relayed the situation over his radio, alerting every other police officer. While Anderson attempted to process the unfolding events, David continued to ramble, his words lost in the chaos. Soon, a reply crackled through the radio:

"We've captured the suspect, a male, under arrest for murder."

Shortly thereafter, an oncology treatment ward was sealed off for investigation following a harrowing incident. Anderson and his colleagues arrived at the scene to confront a disturbing sight that surpassed even their extensive experience. Despite their familiarity with pain and crime, their profession did little to numb the shock of such events, particularly for Anderson, who felt profoundly affected by the murder that had occurred within the confines of his own hospital.

The scene revealed a light grey, leather chair with the lifeless body of a young male seated upon it. He remained tethered to an IV from his treatment, his torso marred by dark blood stains where he had been viciously stabbed. Even the white pillow beneath his arm bore splatters of blood, serving as a grim testament to the violence that had unfolded. Surrounding the tragedy were triangular signs, each numbered from '1' to '6', marking various pieces of evidence.

"Poor lad. Despite all the scenes I've encountered, I still struggle to comprehend what drives people to commit murder," Lily remarked, her voice filled with empathy as she gazed upon the lifeless form before her.

"Every murderer has a motive, and every secret has its price. Some of those secrets we uncover," Ioan reflected solemnly. "But the darkest secrets linger in the shadows, awaiting discovery. If you look closely, you'll find the devil in the details."

"The murderer is the devil himself. To him, murder is merely a game, and the detective, the referee," Anderson added sombrely. "The past fortnight has felt like a game that I'm losing, a sickening game that costs lives."

David, sensing Anderson's despondency, placed a comforting hand on his shoulder. "We've won, Joel. We've won the game."

With those words, a weight lifted from Anderson's shoulders. The murderer had been apprehended, and the chaos had finally abated.

But little did he know, the apprehended culprit was not responsible for the other murders. He remained oblivious to the fact that there were still secrets waiting to be uncovered, potentially endangering more lives.

Chapter 9
Comfortable Desolation.

1:12 PM.

Emma was still shaken from her interview with the police. She was grateful that the interview was only regarding Quinn's murder, rather than Emma being a suspected murderer. As she exited the meeting room, she wasn't surprised to find Ash waiting for her.

"What was that about?" Ash asked.

"Quinn. None of your concerns."

"Do you have the scalpel I asked you for earlier?" She asked. Emma panicked, knowing that if she admitted to forgetting, Ash would make a big deal out of it. She couldn't give Ash a scalpel, she knew Ash would've used it for something malicious. After all, Ash had a bad temper and wasn't afraid to use force.

"Uh, yeah, it's in my bag," Emma said, hoping that a lie would get her out of the situation. She immediately regretted it, not wanting to add more lies to her already-uncomfortable situation.

"You're going on break, right? Get it for me."

Emma couldn't think of another excuse, so she told the truth. "I'm sorry, Ash, I haven't had the time to go get it."

"Not enough time, huh? I thought I'd be able to trust you with such a small task, but I was proven wrong. It's not like I ask for much, is it… But oh well, lucky me." Ash Nagged.

With her heart racing and her nerves on edge, Emma felt the urge to snap at Ash. She had enough of Ash's constant complaints and nagging, and she just wanted to get away from the hospital and Ash for good. She let out a breath and said, "I'm having a bad day, Ash. *Piss off.*"

"Oh, you think you're having a bad day? I've been having a bad day for the past 6 months, and I'm not sat here complaining about it every two seconds!"

Emma couldn't muster any care for Ash's problems. She just wanted to escape both the hospital and Ash, even if it meant going into hiding.

"On top of that, Anderson gave me a lecture about the staff shortage as if it was my fault!"

"Oh, I don't care, Ash! Just shut up, I've had enough, just leave me alone and I'll do whatever you want!"

The words slipped out of Emma's mouth like soap. She didn't even think about what she was saying, and what she said was a mistake. A costly misstep that left her vulnerable to further manipulation and exploitation, this time with her own consent.

Ash let out a snicker at Emma's sudden outburst before responding in a slightly surprised tone, "Alright then. If that's what you want, I'll just be over here enjoying my time while you go on your little quest. Just make sure you get me the scalpel by seven, okay?"

Despite Emma's harsh words, Ash had a smug and almost amused expression on her face, as if she had gotten what she wanted. She knew that Emma was under her control and would do whatever she told her to. The thought of having such power over someone made Ash feel invincible.

With frustration in her voice, Emma said, "Fine, deal."

Making a deal with Ash felt like making a deal with the devil. In surrendering herself like a captive on an unbreakable chain, Emma had, in essence, traded her soul away to Ash.

Ash took a step forward as if she were about to leave, but then turned around abruptly. "Ah, before I go, don't you dare even think about using that sort of language on me again or you'll find out what silence truly sounds like."

'What does that even mean?!' Emma wondered as Ash walked away. She didn't know how to respond, was that a threat? Because it sent

chills down Emma's spine. Her words always do, its like dark magic, taking over Emma's brain like poison after every interaction.

'She's gone now. I'm alone. I'm safe.'

Shortly thereafter, Emma found herself in the staff room, holding a freshly brewed coffee she had prepared herself. For the moment, she was alone in the room, though she knew it wouldn't last long as her colleagues would soon trickle in for their breaks.

The accumulated stress of the week weighed heavily on her shoulders. The idea of returning to the chaotic flurry of caring for countless patients left her feeling drained. All Emma yearned for was someone else to extend a caring hand to her for once. But nobody did. Nobody cared. Nobody listened, nobody empathised, nobody understood. After all, she was just a nurse, wasn't she? Surely, she was expected to have it all together. She had to be fine, for how could she care for others if she couldn't care for herself? That expectation seemed absurd.

She's *just* a nurse.

Emma glanced around the room, seeking refuge from the tumult of the day. It was a familiar scene; one she had witnessed far too often. She was sick of it. A day that dragged on, with nobody there to offer solace, only a relentless headache pounding against the walls of her skull.

Silence enveloped her. Normally, she would welcome the peace it offered, a rare break from the cacophony of her thoughts and Ash's incessant nagging. But today, she craved anything but that silence. She longed for a comforting voice to fill the void, to reassure her that everything would be alright. Opting to call her parents instead, she hoped for their soothing words.

No answer.

It felt like another straw had been plucked from the bundle, like a game of kerplunk where each straw represented a fragment of her composure. With every passing moment, the weight of the marbles grew heavier, threatening to topple the delicate balance she had maintained. One by one, the straws snapped or were yanked away until, inevitably, the marbles cascaded down, plunging Emma into a pit of shattered darkness.

She took a deep breath, cradling the warm cup of coffee in her hands. Coffee wasn't her favourite, but in moments of stress like this, it served as a comforting anchor.

"It's just a bad day, Emma." She murmured, like ice soothing a wound until she could retreat home and put the day behind her.

"Things will get better. They always do." Those are the words Rosa would tell her during these stressful shifts and her own bad days, and it was true. Things always improve; for most people, that is. Emma believed that if you look for the bright things in life, you'll find them. Others that ignore them won't. That's the difference between her and Ash. She would always find the bright side of life, Ash never will.

After the coffee cooled, Emma took a sip, anticipating warmth but recoiling at the unexpected bitterness.

'...*bitter...? Why is it—*'

Emma's eyes widened with horror as she realized what she had just done. She hastily spit out the coffee, her mouth full of the bitter taste, and threw the rest of the cup across the room. It shattered across the floor, adding to the already-chaotic scene.

'The bastard poisoned it. She fucking poisoned me.'

Ash lied. She said she was only going to poison the one jar, she promised there would only be one victim.

'Will I be the next victim...? Who else is she going to kill without me knowing?!'

A whirlwind of thoughts spun through her head, each more frantic than the last. The spilt, boiling coffee burnt her skin through her clothes, her heart thundered against her chest, her breaths came in gasps. It was too much. The final straw had been pulled and she completely lost control of herself.

Emma's heart raced like a wild stallion, pounding against her ribcage so fiercely, she's sure it'll burst through her chest. Every breath feels like it's being sucked out of her lungs by an invisible vacuum, leaving her gasping for air as if she's drowning on dry land.

Her palms grew clammy, fingers trembling uncontrollably as if possessed by some unseen force. Sweat beads formed on her forehead despite the chill in the air, trickling down her temples in rivulets, leaving a trail of icy fear in her wake.

The room around her begins to blur, edges melting into a hazy fog that swallows everything whole. Sounds distort, becoming muffled and distant, as if she's trapped underwater with no way to surface. Even the familiar sights had become alien and menacing.

The door creaked open as Charlotte stepped into the room, but Emma remained oblivious to her presence, lost in the turmoil of her own thoughts. The woman's steps were drowned out by the cacophony of Emma's hyperventilation, a symphony of panic that filled the space.

Instantly observing Emma's distressed state, Charlotte felt compelled to intervene despite their strained relationship. She approached Emma cautiously, her voice carrying a soothing tone.

"Hey..." She said with a gentle voice. "Hey, it's alright, you're okay, Emma. You're safe."

Emma couldn't focus on Charlotte, all she could focus on was the feeling of her chest tighten and the terrifying sound of each heartbeat reverberating through her entire being, echoing like a death knell in the cavernous depths of her mind. She clutched at her chest, nails digging into her skin, desperate to alleviate the suffocating pressure that threatens to consume her whole.

"Emma." Charlotte urged, a bit louder than earlier. "Look at me."

Emma continued to hunch over, her shoulders and her skin tacky with a sheen of sweat. It wasn't until Charlotte placed her hand on Emma's that she looked up from her chest. She finally met the blonde's gentle gaze, the first step towards breaking free from the glass cage that had trapped her within her own mind. The simple gesture of Charlotte placing her hand on Emma' a was enough for her to feel a spark of hope, to see a way out.

"You're having a panic attack, Emma. Let's focus on your breathing, okay?"

Charlotte guided Emma through calming techniques, patiently coaxing her back from the brink of overwhelming panic. Gradually, Emma's racing heart slowed, though she remained visibly shaken and drained. Charlotte offered her water, recognizing the aftermath of Emma's attack, like it's something she's experienced many times before.

As Emma took hesitant sips, her demeanour spoke volumes of her vulnerability and exhaustion. The way she rocked forwards and backwards while fiddling with her hands made her look as if she had no idea what to do with herself.

Charlotte, ever patient, inquired if Emma wanted to talk, receiving a subtle shake of the head in response.

Undeterred, Charlotte tore a piece of paper from her notebook, jotting down her number before passing it to Emma. "I understand this is overwhelming, but I'm here for you. Whether it's a walk or just a chat, let me know if you need someone."

With a gentle offer of support, Charlotte left the door open for Emma to reach out when ready, a silent promise of solidarity in their shared struggle.

7:20 PM.

Ash returned home from her shift, seething with frustration. Despite the late hour, the scalpel she'd requested from Emma remained elusive. She spent the last 20 minutes of her shift storming around the hospital, searching for the brunette, but she was nowhere to be seen. On top of that, the memory of the family she encountered earlier in her shift lingered, boiling her blood. Even her macabre "murder game" failed to provide the distraction she craved, no deaths, no progress in the investigation. At least, none that she knew of.

'That fucking idiot.' Ash seethed inwardly. *'She hid from me, how dare she. One thing I asked for, one thing, and she couldn't even get that right.'*

After drawing the curtains shut, she retreated to the kitchen, snatching a bottle of whiskey from the cabinet before slumping into the sofa. With a thud, the bottle landed on the coffee table before her, a silent companion in her frustration.

Fingers trembling with agitation, she flicked on the TV, drowning out the silence with the murmur of a late-night show. She took out her phone, hoping for a message off Emma regarding the scalpel, only to find an empty screen which read, "No new notifications," prompting her to hurl the device across the room in a fit of indignation.

With shaky hands, she reached for the whiskey bottle, its cool surface a balm to her frayed nerves. Unscrewing the cap released the familiar scent of alcohol, a sharp reminder of her chosen escape.

Rasing the bottle to her lips, she took a long, deliberate sip. The liquid burned as it slid down her throat, igniting a fire within her chest that momentarily dulled the ache in her soul.

How she loved that sting.

Another sip, and another, each one bringing her closer to that elusive state of numbness she craved. With each swallow, the world around her seemed to fade away, leaving the comforting embrace of intoxication in its wake. Alcohol was her painkiller, her escape from reality. It was the temporary filling that filled the hole shaped like Ellie. It was the only thing that could make a cold-blooded woman's blood warm.

The taste of the whiskey danced on her tongue, a sharp contrast to the dull ache of sorrow that had become her constant companion. It was a bitter sweetness, a reminder that even in her darkest moments, there was still pleasure to be found, however fleeting it may be.

As the alcohol took hold, Ash felt herself begin to relax, the tension draining from her muscles as a sense of euphoria wash over her. For a brief, beautiful moment, she was free from the weight of her grief, free from the crushing despair that threatened to consume her whole.

But there was one thing missing.

A cigarette.

With the bottle in one hand, she picked up the half-full packet of cigarettes and placed a cigarette in her mouth, holding it in between her teeth.

The flame of her lighter flickered to life, casting dancing shadows across her face as she took the first deep drag.

The first drag was always the best. It makes the world disappear, replacing it with a rush of warmth that flooded her senses. She could feel the euphoric feeling in her blood, flowing through her body, allowing her to forget the troubles of her life, allowing her to relax.

It felt like the end of a shift.

It felt like Ellie's grave.

It felt like a murder.

As she exhaled slowly, the tendrils of smoke curled upwards, disappearing into the air.

Closing her eyes with a smile, Ash savoured the taste of the cigarette, the sharp tang mingling with the sweetness of nostalgia and comforting desolation. With each inhale, she felt her body melt into the couch beneath her.

Another gulp of the whiskey.

Another drag of the cigarette.

Like lemon and lime, like peanut butter and jelly, like coffee and cyanide.

It was a perfect match.

7:20 PM.

The moment Emma stepped into her apartment, she reached for the phone and dialled her parent's number, eager to share them about her day. Though she skirted around the details, not wanting to burden them with worries, she told them enough to hear them say, *"You're strong, Emma. We're proud of what you do, and we couldn't be more grateful to have you as our daughter."*

Their unwavering support meant everything to her. She loved her parents more than sleep, more than mint-flavoured chocolate, even more than Rosa. They had been her steadfast companions through her every highlight and downfall, and their presence was her favourite source of comfort and strength.

Her thoughts turned briefly to her sister; their bond unbroken save for childhood squabbles. Together, they weathered life's storms until tragedy struck in the form of a fatal car accident. Emma still mourned her loss, but she had learned to carry on, buoyed by the memories they shared.

Encouraged by her parents, Emma contemplated finding comfort by talking to someone, considering the walk with Charlotte. Despite their strained relationship, Charlotte had been the only comforting presence during Emma's panic attack.

On the other hand, Ash proved that just because someone says something, doesn't mean you're necessarily 'friends.' Unfortunately, Emma learnt that the hard way. Despite that, Emma hesitated briefly before reaching for the slip of paper Charlotte had given her earlier, her fingers hovering over her phone's screen.

There was a chance they might clash, but there was also the possibility of getting along. Emma held onto that glimmer of hope, recognizing that sometimes, bridges could be rebuilt, and wounds could heal with time.

With a mixture of hope and apprehension, she composed a message, willing to take the risk for the possibility of a fresh start.

Twenty minutes later, they found themselves strolling through a local park – a different one from where Emma had discovered Quinn's body, of course. The path ahead was illuminated by warm streetlights, casting a cozy and comforting glow over their surroundings. Despite ethe chilly air nipping at their noses, their snug coats, hands and gloves, shielded them from the biting cold.

"Thank you… for helping me earlier." Emma murmured beneath her coat. "I don't know what happened, I completely lost control of myself."

"You're welcome, I'm just glad I could be there for you," Charlotte replied warmly. "Do you… want to talk about it?"

Emma hesitated before opening up about the whirlwind of stress engulfing her life. "Life's just been so stressful lately. Work, mental health, it's all been chaos…"

"I know what you mean. You're work in emergency medicine too, right?"

Emma nodded. "Triage, too."

"I know how busy the emergency room can get, especially during the wintertime." Said Charlotte.

Emma discussed the overwhelming burden of taking care of so many people on her own, not having anyone to support her in the process, and her struggles to cope with the situations. And,

"And Ash."

"Ash?"

"Yeah. *God, she stresses me out.*"

Charlotte chuckled without realizing the severity of the situation. "Is she really that bad?"

"She can be awful." Emma started. "I'm probably being dramatic, but she makes me feel awful sometimes."

Charlotte was taken aback by Emma's revelations. Despite not witnessing much interaction between the two, she had assumed they were close friends. "I'm so sorry, I had no idea she was like that," she responded sympathetically.

As Emma detailed Ash's behaviour – without revealing anything she shouldn't have, Charlotte listened carefully, though she struggled to discern the specifics of the tasks Emma referred to. Assuming they were typical hostile duties like cleaning and organizing, Charlotte empathized, knowing well the burden of such responsibilities. Little did she know, the 'tasks' Emma was thinking about were the heartless tasks of taking lives and harming patients.

"She lashes out a lot when she's mad." Said Emma. "It feels like I'm being controlled by pressure and anxiety. If I do something wrong, if I'm pushed to the edge, I don't know if I'll be safe."

"Wow, that sounds awful," Charlotte remarked, unsure of what else to say.

Emma nodded in agreement. "It is, especially after a life has been lost." Said Emma. "She blames it on me. It makes me feel… like…"

Their conversation lapsed into a contemplative silence before Charlotte shifted gears, offering a sincere apology for her past behaviour. Confessing her jealousy and misguided attempts to win Ash's favour, Charlotte expressed remorse for her actions.

"I was jealous of you. I wanted to be Ash's favourite, and to do that, I tried to take your place. Turns out she's not all that good, and you're the one I should've been trying to impress."

Emma smiled, appreciating the honesty. "Thank you for the apology. I appreciate it."

"You're welcome. Forgive me?"

"I forgive you."

Charlotte smiled. "How about we start off fresh? I'm Charlotte Hyle. I love ice cream, my cat Luna, and my boyfriend, Ryan, but I hate mushrooms."

"You have a boyfriend?!" Emma laughed, surprised by the revelation of Charlotte's relationship. She was even more surprised when Charlotte announced that they've been together for 6 years.

"Okay, I'm Emma Middleton. I love mint chocolate, baking and helping other people, but I hate spiders. A lot." Emma shared in return.

Charlotte placed out her hand for a handshake. "Nice to meet you, Emma."

"Really? A handshake?" Emma laughed.

"Isn't that what you're supposed to do? I don't know!"

As Emma shook Charlotte's hand, she noticed a light pink, silicone bracelet, with the word 'ASTHMA' written on it.

"You have asthma?" Emma asked curiously.

Looking at the band, Charlotte replied, "Yeah, unfortunately it gets pretty bad at times, so I keep this on while in public."

"Oh, wow. I've learnt a lot about you today."

"Right? Tell me more about yourself."

The two women continued walking through the park, lost in conversation about everything and nothing at the same time. Emma felt a sense of relief in finally having someone to get along with, someone to talk to, a person who made her feel seen, understood, and valued. After so many lonely days, it was a welcome change to have someone confide in and share her struggles with, someone who would listen without judgement and be a source of emotional support.

Maybe things do get better.

9:50 PM.

The cigarette, once a flickering flame of solace, now lay abandoned in the ashtray among the other spent butts. Ash's ritual was familiar: finish one cigarette, then reach for another, much like a child in a sweet shop, she couldn't resist the allure of another treat. The same pattern applied to her alcohol consumption, she'd finish one bottle and stumble to the kitchen for another, a relentless cycle of indulgence regardless of any self-imposed limits. After all, why stop when the night was meant for enjoyment?

But she was no longer having a good time.

Ash was a heavy drinker, but on her worse days, she'd end up like this. Huddled on the cold, tiled bathroom floor, her body racked with violent tremors as she retched into the toilet bowl.

Each heave sent waves of nausea crashing over her, a relentless onslaught that left her gasping for breath. The taste of bile mixed with nicotine lingered on her tongue, a reminder that she put herself in this situation. And she knew she would. She knew tonight was going to be a heavy night, and she knew drinking the night before a morning shift was the worst thing she could do.

But *'fuck it'.* When does she ever get to have fun? When is the only time she's free from envy, guilt and regret?

When she's drinking. While her nights typically don't usually end in such turmoil, and as horrible it might make her feel, the small amount of time the fleeting escape from reality feels worthwhile despite the ensuing discomfort. Indeed, the aftermath of her indulgence pales in comparison to the emotional agony she seeks to numb. The difference is stark: when sober, she's inundated with every dreadful emotion imaginable.

Ash understands that physical pain fades with time, but the anguish of losing her daughter lingers indefinitely. No medication or treatment can assuage that deep-seated sorrow.

Nothing can bring back her daughter.

Pain is pain, but mental anguish cuts deep and lasts long after the physical wounds have long healed.

Today, however, the physical toll is particularly severe. The dimly lighted bathroom around her was blurred and spun around her. Her entire head felt like it was going to explode through her skull.

After her sickness passed, she stood up slowly, feeling her pounding head blur her vision even more. She bent over the sink and used her hands to splash her face with the icy water, but when she stood back up, through the mirror, she could hardly recognize the hollow eyes that stared back at her. It was ghostly, distorted by pain and regret.

She couldn't even recognize herself.

When she glanced back at the sink, Ash noticed the empty gap in the toothbrush holder, one which used to hold two toothbrushes. A small, pink toothbrush, but now only her toothbrush remained. Only her shampoo stood solitary next to the shower, only her towel hung alone from the hook on the door.

In the hallway, a young girl's shoes which were never to be worn again. There were no barbie dolls scattered around the house, no loud giggles, no stuffed animals, no drawings on the walls. Just furniture, empty glass bottles, ash trays, and a woman, existing in a cold silence.

Ash looked back into the mirror, gripping onto the edges of the sink.

'It's my fault. It's all my fucking fault.'

The anger quickly rose within her as she felt a new emotion.

Shame.

She felt ashamed. Completely embarrassed. The person that stared back at Ash through the mirror was *her*. She was the reason that Ellie died. She is the reason why she will never be a mother. She is the reason why everybody left her, why nobody cares, why she can't get help, why she can't help herself.

Rage pulsed through her veins propelling her to lash out. With a primal scream, she slammed her fist into the mirror, shattering it into a thousand shards.

"Fuck, fuck, fuck!" She groaned in pain as she quickly examined her hand. A few of the glass segments had cut through her knuckles and hand, leaving small, bloody cuts, which throbbed in pain.

Stumbling into the living room, fuelled by adrenaline and fury, Ash unleashed her pent-up rage upon the surroundings. She overturned furniture, shattered glass, and screamed obscenities into the void.

She swept her arm across the coffee table, sending the empty bottles crashing to the floor. The sound of shattering echoed through the house as ash trays met their demise against the unforgiving surface.

As her tantrum continued, furniture was overturned, items were tossed around the room, cushions were torn asunder in her frenzy, while she shouted things like, *"You fucking asshole," "You took away my life," "I hate you."*

But Ash didn't even know who it was that she despised so desperately. Images of Quinn, Charlie, Kat, all the people she's ever hated, filled her mind. But one image stood out the most.

The image of herself.

The once comfortable home of a mother and child now resembled a battlefield, strewn with the debris of rage. Laying in the middle of the battlefield was Ash. Her chest heaved with each ragged breath after she surveyed the chaos she had wrought. Guilt gnawed at her conscience, a nagging reminder of the consequences of her actions.

The only thing that remained perfectly unharmed was the picture of Ellie, framed in a pink picture frame.

Ash picked up the picture and stared at it in silence. Then, a warm, wet droplet slid down her cheek.

She thought that she had cried all her tears, and all that was left was anger. But she proved herself wrong as she burst into tears.

Apologies spilled from her lips in whispered pleas as remorse flooded her soul. "I'm sorry. I'm sorry, I'm sorry, I'm sorry…" she repeated, her voice choked with emotion.

"I couldn't keep you save. I couldn't... I'm..." She cried. "The hospital couldn't save you... I wanted to... See you grow old... But I couldn't." Another sob ripped through her throat. "I'm not going to make that same mistake again... Lend me the life you had and lend it to Evelyn. I'll let her live a good life, I promise, she'll have the life I couldn't give you."

As midnight approached, her outrageous, drunken cries soon died into smaller sobs. She eventually fell to sleep, still in her scrubs, still clinging to the image of her lost daughter.

It was still a warzone, but for now, it was comfortable desolation.

Chapter 10
No longer human.

The trees rustled with a static sound, battling against the rough wind that pushed through their branches. Raindrops raced down the window as a result of the harsh stormy weather outside. Ash was sitting on the baby-blue leather chair, positioned across from ~~her daughter, Ellie Evelyn's~~ – A young girl's hospital bed. The girl had light, brown hair, pale skin, but her face was… Blurred.

A cacophony of beeps pierced Ash's skull like a relentless assault on her senses. Figures materialized from the shadows, their faces twisted and blurred. Within those figures was Emma and Quinn.

Quinn's form materialized, her movements jerky and disjointed, as if controlled by unseen forces. She pressed down on the bed with a violence that shook the room as she performed chest compressions.

In the corner of the room, Charlie stood, his presence casting a shadow that seemed to devour the light. Beside him, a blonde woman in a white wedding dress, her face constantly shifting from someone Ash recognized to a blur.

In Charlie's arms lay a lifeless infant, its features twisted and displaced. The greyish, deceased infant cried loudly, adding another layer of horror to the already stressful situation. Somehow, Ash knew the newborn was Arthur, despite seeing his face.

The young girl on the bed screamed, her voice aberrant amalgamation of past and present. "Mommy, don't leave me! I don't want to go, make it stop!" she wailed, her words a desperate plea that clawed at Ash's soul.

Ash cried across the racket, "I know, baby… I'm trying to save you! Please don't leave me… I need you…"

Charlie's voice cut through the screams like a blade, his accusations ringing the weight of centuries. "You killed them," he spat, his words a venomous accusation that searched Ash's very soul. "You killed my children, you're a heartless murderer!"

The young girl's screams reached a fever pitch, her voice a symphony of pain and terror. Ash reached out to comfort her, but her hands grasped only empty air. Suddenly, Quinn's appearance underwent a sudden transformation. Her crisp, clean doctor's uniform abruptly transformed into a blood-soaked, blue and white shirt – the very clothing she wore on the day Ash brutally murdered her. With a flick of her wrist, she raised a bloodied hammer, it swung suddenly, then…

Ash startled awake, her heart pounding like a drum in her chest, her breaths shallow and rapid. It was yet another nightmare, a recurring torment that haunted her nights. Each one had the same eerie familiarity, a twisted tapestry of blurred faces and overwhelming dread that left her shaken upon waking. Despite their nonsensical nature, they felt chillingly real. Sometimes, Ash would struggle to tell the nightmares and real-life apart.

Carefully, Ash sat up, her head throbbing as if it really were struck with a hammer. She rubbed her eyes, searching for her phone to check the time, only to find it elusively out of reach in the dimly lit room. The remnants of broken whiskey bottles littered the floor, a reminder of the chaos that had unfolded.

Surveying the destruction around her, Ash couldn't help but feel a surge of disbelief. "What the hell happened…?" she muttered to herself; her voice tinged with exhaustion. For a fleeing moment, the boundaries between dream and wakefulness blurred, leaving her disoriented and uncertain.

Ash finally retrieved her phone to find the early hour glaring back at her: 4:58 AM. With a weary sigh, she faced a choice: succumb to the pull of sleep or confront the darkness that lurked within her own mind.

Opting for the latter, Ash reached for her notebook, concealed beneath the sofa, its pages filled with the gruesome details of her secret plans. With a determined flick of her pen, she began to sketch out a new strategy, her plan to save Evelyn from the hospital. To keep her alive and safe.

To undo the mistake of failing Ellie.

January 17th, 10:30 AM

After her heart-to-heart conversation with Charlotte the previous night, Emma felt a weight lifted off her shoulders. She spent the night baking a strawberries and cream cake for Rosa, planning to visit her the next morning. Remembering Rosa's love for the dessert, Emma saw it was a small gesture of comfort for her grieving friend.

"Okay, cake's ready, phones on hand...," Emma muttered to herself as she prepared to step out. Just then, her phone began to ring.

Seeing Ash's name displayed on the screen, Emma hesitated to answer. She knew the conversation was unlikely to be pleasant. Yet, aware that ignoring Ash would only delay the inevitable confrontation, she reluctantly answered the call.

"Hello, Ash—"

"Where were you last night?" Ash's voice crackled with frustration through the phone.

"I... I uhm, I had to leave work early."

"No, you didn't. You hid from me because you didn't get me my scalpel."

Emma struggled to find the right words as Ash's tirade continued, each accusation. Despite knowing not to allow Ash's words to bother her, she could feel the sting of Ash's words cutting deep.

"One thing I wanted, and you couldn't do it? Not a simple task? I thought maybe I could trust you, but noooo, you prove me wrong, didn't you?"

'That red hang-up button looks great right now...' Emma thought.

"I'll just have to get the fucking thing myself, won't I? You useless piece of shit."

Eventually, Ash hung up in a strop. Emma had learnt to not let her words affect her, but hearing her harsh voice still stung like a whip.

Stuffing her phone back into her pocket, Emma took a deep breath and whispered,

"Alright, let's go."

Visiting Rosa had been on Emma's mind for a while, but she wasn't sure when to visit, or if Rosa even wanted her there. Now, standing outside Rosa's front door with a box containing the cake she had baked, Emma felt a mix of anticipation and uncertainty. Everything had gone perfectly. Daniel was no more, Rosa was safe—what could possibly go wrong from here? Emma could now speak openly with her dear friend, finally ready to confess her feelings, anticipating that they might be reciprocated, and then—

"Oh hey, Gem," Rosa greeted as she swung open the front door, catching Emma lost in thought. With a warm smile, Emma welcomed Rosa inside.

Emma felt a sense of familiarity as she walked into the house, having been there a few times before. It was a sharp contrast to Ash's home, both of them navigating the labyrinth of grief in their own ways.

Rosa's house had a clean, modern feeling. The centrepiece was a plush grey sofa adorned with navy blue cushions and a matching fleece throw. Light wooden floors were complemented by a soft white mat, and a sleek white coffee table stood proudly in the centre. A modern painting hung above the sofa, opposite a sleek television.

As Emma settled onto the sofa, Rosa entered the room holding cups of coffee and tea, along with utensils for the cake.

"You really didn't have to bake a cake for me, Gem." Rosa said softly as she began to serve slices of cake. "But I appreciate it. You know strawberries and cream are my weakness."

"I know I'm not great with emotions, but I hoped this would bring you some comfort," Emma replied. They shared a moment over their cake before Emma broached the topic on her mind.

"How have you been holding up?" Emma asked gently.

Rosa's smile faltered, her eyes betraying the pain she carried. "Not too great, honestly. I miss Daniel. A lot."

Emma nodded empathetically. "Yeah, grieving is never easy." She offered.

Their conversation took a more serious turn as Emma delicately addressed her concerns about Daniel's treatment of Rosa. She recounted Ash's observations from the party and Daniel's overall behaviour, hoping to shed light on Rosa's relationship.

Rosa listened, her expression shifting from surprise to contemplation. "I did have my doubts," she admitted, her voice tinged with regret. "But I loved him. I didn't want to see the truth."

Drawing closer, Emma placed a comforting hand on Rosa's knee. "I'm sorry things ended this way," she said softly. "But you deserve to be cherished, respected and loved."

A flicker of hope ignited in Emma's heart as she looked into Rosa's eyes. "And I can do that for you," she added, her voice tinged with sincerity.

Rosa paused, her mind reeling with confusion as she tried to work out Emma's intentions. Was Emma simply expressing platonic affection, or was there something more beneath her words?

"Emma, what do you mean?" Rosa's voice held a hint of concern, unsure of what Emma's confession might entail. She knew Emma was bisexual, but she hadn't anticipated…

"I like you, Rosa."

Emma's declaration hung in the air, uttered with a mix of nervousness and relief. It was a moment Emma had been building up to for so long, a confession of her true feelings for her closest friend. Yet, Rosa's response shattered the fragile hop that had been swelling within her.

"I…" Rosa's voice trailed off, grappling for the right words. "Emma, I'm sorry…"

Emma physically felt her heart skip a beat at those two words.

No.

This is not how it was supposed to go.

"You're one of the kindest people I've ever met, Emma, and I think you're amazing, but…" Rosa's voice faltered, the weight of her words sinking in. "I love you like a friend, like family. But I can't love you the way I love Daniel."

Emma's silence belied the storm of emotions raging within her. She had endured so much, sacrificed so deeply, all in the hope of winning

Rosa's affection. And now, faced with rejection, a different emotion began to surface.

"You wouldn't be able to love me the way you love Daniel." Emma quietly repeated, her tone tinged with anger, almost threatening.

"No, I mean- I worded it wrong, Emma, I—"

Emma brushed off Rosa's explanation, sensing its inadequacy. But apologies seemed futile now; a monstrous realization was closing in on Emma's consciousness with relentless speed, leaving no room for regrets or amends.

"Do you know what I did for you, Rosa?" Emma's voice was low, avoiding Rosa's gaze. "Do you understand how much bullshit I went through just to make you happy? To keep you safe?"

Tension crackled between them as Emma poured out her feelings, her frustration, her sacrifices. Rosa attempted to interject, to explain, but Emma's fury brooked no interruption. It was a side of Emma that Rosa had never witnessed, a dark, unfamiliar side of her friend that now stood before her like a stranger.

"I cried, I worried, I suffered for you, Rosa." Emma continued, her words escalating with each moment. "I saw the dangers and I took action. I poisoned bastard to protect you, and this is how you repay me?!"

Rosa's eyes widened in disbelief. *'Did I hear that correctly...?'* But fear rooted her to the spot, rendering her unable to speak. She dreaded knowing the answer, yet the truth unfolded before her eyes as the demon within Emma seized control of her subconsciousness.

"You're unbelievable! I can't fucking believe you, you traitor!" Emma's voice rang out, charged with fury, as she lunged forward and grabbed the knife on the coffee table. She plunged the knife into Rosa's stomach without a second thought, just above her intestines.

A harrowing scream tore from Rosa's lips as the blade penetrated her flesh, followed by another as it was forcibly withdrawn. Emma stood across from her, the bloodied knife clutched at her side, as Rosa's cries served as a stark reminder of the gruesome reality that had unfolded.

Emma's trance was shattered by the cacophony of Rosa's agony, jolting her back to the present moment. The enormity of what she had done crashed over her like a tidal wave, leaving her stunned and incapable of comprehending her actions. She was both physically and mentally paralyzed, grappling with the incomprehensible truth that she had just stabbed her best friend, her crush, the person she loved.

The bloody knife remained in her grasp, a damning testament to her unfathomable deed. Meanwhile, Rosa writhed in agony, her cries echoing through the room, a piercing symphony of pain.

"Oh my god… Oh my god, oh my god, oh my god, Rosa- I—" Emma's words tumbled out in a panic, but Rosa could only cry out in anguish, the pain radiating from the wound in her stomach overwhelming her senses. It felt like being pummelled in the gut, the searing sensation of the blade burning through her skin and flesh sending shockwaves of agony through her body.

In a frantic bid to stem the bleeding, Emma scanned the room for anything that could help. Her eyes fell on the fleece throw draped over the couch, and she seized it, pressing it tightly against Rosa's wound in a desperate attempt to staunch the flow of blood.

The gut-wrenching groan that escaped Rosa's lips under the sudden pressure made Emma feel sick to her core. "I'm sorry Rosa, I'm so sorry, I know it hurts, but I have to save you, I can't—"

"You stabbed me…" Rosa voice was barely a whisper, heavy with betrayal. "I… Trusted you…"

Emma's panicked sobs filled the air as she stumbled over her words, a torrent of meaningless apologies tumbling from her lips. She knew time was the essence, but her mind was a chaotic whirlwind of guilt and remorse.

"You never truly know someone... Even your closest friend." Rosa murmured, her voice trembling with anger and pain.

"I'm sorry, I'm sorry, I'm sorry, I'm sorry, I'm sorry..." Emma's desperate refrain echoed in the room, but her tears and apologies were futile, wasting precious time.

Rosa's distress escalated, her heart heavy with devastation. As her body began to succumb to the cold grip of mortality, her vision blurred, and a chill swept over her. Yet, in this fleeting moment of clarity, she grasped onto Emma's earlier words about Ash. With her final breaths, she mustered the strength to utter, "Report Ash... to the police... And yourself. Get help, Emma... Stay... s-safe."

Emma's heart clenched as she watched Rosa's condition deteriorate rapidly. Rosa's face went pale and ice-cold, her breaths becoming shallower by the second. "Stay with me, Rose, please..." Emma pleaded, her voice choked with grief.

"D-don't... Call me... Rose."

Those haunting words marked Rosa's final breaths. Emma's world shattered as she witnessed Rosa slip away, leaving her alone in a nightmare of her own making. She wept broken apologies to Rosa, begging for forgiveness that would never come.

Emma wept uncontrollably as tears cascaded down her cheeks, whispering broken apologies to Rosa, pleading for her to hold on. But it was futile. Rosa's grip on life slipped away like sand through her fingers, leaving Emma stranded in her own nightmare that she once called 'life.'

Emma could no longer recognize herself. Not as the kind human being she used to be, but a murderer. A ruthless killer. She couldn't blame Rosa's death on Ash's manipulation, it wasn't caused by fate, it was all Emma.

An act she would *never* forgive herself for.

An act that made her no longer human.

Emma's sobs made it feel like her throat had been ripped open by burning, sharp claws, and everything became blurry because of tears. She was gagging from her own sobs. Drowning in tears, she struggled to gasp for air. But Emma didn't care about her wet cheeks, her runny nose or anything for that matter. All she wanted was to save Rosa, but seeing Rosa's skin turn cold and grey, she knew Rosa was beyond saving.

Emma collapsed into another tsunami of tears on top of Rosa, feeling her clothes soak up Rosa's blood. The thought of calling an ambulance didn't occur to her once, she just kept repeating the words, *'I'm sorry, I'm sorry, I'm sorry, I'm sorry, I'm sorry...'* in her head, as she couldn't physically say the words out loud.

Emma's tears flowed for another twenty agonizing minutes until she resolved to halt Ash's reign of terror once and for all. Reflecting on the grim reality, she realized that had she never crossed paths with Ash, she would likely be toiling alongside her best friend in the hospital at that very moment. Quinn would still be alive. Rosa would still be alive. Daniel, Kat, Justin—all would have been spared. Yet, it was Emma's actions that sealed their fates.

She could have intervened. She could have halted Ash's destructive path with ease. Emma had numerous opportunities to alert the authorities, to confront Ash, to compel her to seek help. But she faltered. She succumbed to Ash's manipulation and threats, and as a result, she bore the weight of their tragic demise.

Everyone she ever cared for is gone.

"Even in your last moments, you deserve to be comfortable." Emma whispered between wet sniffles, her voice thick with sorrow. Gently, she repositioned Rosa's body on the couch, carefully tucking the fleece throw around her, allowing Rosa's serene face to be visible. With delicate movements, she adjusted the cushion under Rosa's head, creating the illusion of peaceful slumber amidst the chaos of the murder scene.

As Emma moved the pillow, her tear-blurred vision caught sight of something tucked behind it. Through the haze of her grief, she struggled to discern its shape, initially mistaking it for a mundane object. However, as she wiped her eyes and focused, realization dawned like a thunderbolt.

It was a pregnancy test.

The implications hit Emma like a physical blow. Two distinct lines marked the test, unmistakably indicating pregnancy. Rosa, she realized, had been carrying a child, a secret she had intended to share with Emma at the right moment.

In that moment, Emma's heart seemed to cease its beating. The weight of her actions crashed down upon her with unbearable force. In her reckless desperation, she had not only taken Rosa's life but also that of her unborn child.

The enormity of the tragedy engulfed Emma, suffocating her with guilt and remorse. She sank to her knees, consumed by the devastating realization that her actions had shattered not one, but two lives.

11:45 AM

The weather quickly shifted from cloudy to a violent rainstorm, its relentless taps echoing throughout the hospital. Emma, having changed into her scrubs, returned to the hospital with a clear mission: to confront Ash. Ash would either turn herself in, or Emma forcibly drag her to the police herself.

Despite scouring the entire hospital without finding Ash, Emma knew exactly where she might be. Climbing the stairway to the fourth floor, she braced herself for the daunting task ahead. The mere thought of facing Ash on the rooftop made her palms sweat with nervous anticipation. She knew Ash was angry, especially after hiding from her the day before, and she had no idea what would happen. Maybe Ash would continue to drag Emma through her shit, maybe she would kill Emma.

Or, perhaps Emma's plan would finally win Ash over, and the two would be arrested, just like Rosa wanted. But that's not going to happen if Emma continues to linger nervously at the staircase, staring through the small window at Ash, who was standing dangerously close to the edge in the pouring rain.

'Has she gone insane?! It's soaking wet out here!' Emma thought as she approached the rooftop.

"Ash!" she shouted from a safe distance, away from Ash, who turned around at the call. "What are you doing out here, you're soaking!"

The way Ash stared at Emma sent shivers down her spine, though she couldn't quite pinpoint what was different. Suppressing her rising anxiety, Emma remained composed, knowing that Ash thrived on her fear.

"This hospital is nothing but a death trap." Ash declared. "Everyone here is evil. They don't care about lives. They don't care about mothers and their children. They killed Ellie and they're going to kill Evelyn too, and they're going to blame it on me. I'm not going to make the same mistake twice."

Emma attempted to reason with her. "I know you love Evelyn, but she's not Ellie. Ellie is gone, and you need to accept that. *You are not Evelyn's mother.*"

"I know," Ash conceded, her resolve unwavering. "But I can still protect her. That's why we're going to burn this hospital down along with the devils inside it. I'm going to save Evelyn and send every other fucker to hell."

Emma's demeanour turned icy.

"What's wrong, Emma? Something's made your eyes go cold."

Emma's mind raced as she thought about Charlotte and April, her two friends that were being put in danger. She thought about Rosa. She thought about Kat, Daniel, Justin.

She thought about Quinn.

"The day Quinn died, I made a promise to myself that I would find the strength to keep going, no matter how hard it might be. When Rosa died in my arms, I promised that I'd end your chaos once and for all."

"Rosa?" Ash scoffed. "What did you do to the poor bastard. Did you kill her, too?"

Emma hesitated, grappling with the weight of her actions. If she was already a murderer, then what harm would it do to eliminate the main problem?

"You're not going to stop me. You're too weak. You're going to help me. After all, no one expects an angel to set the world on fire."

'*I am not weak. I am not fucking weak.*' Ash's taunts ignited a surge of adrenaline within Emma, fuelling her with a potent mix of power and rage.

"Go to hell!" Emma's voice reverberated as she shoved Ash with all her might. Ash stumbled backward, but Emma realized her mistake too late.

They weren't close enough to the edge.

Ash hit the ground with a thud, her smile twisted into one of pure malice.

"Where do you think I came from?" Ash hissed, her hand creeping into her pocket. "And I'm going to go back, and I'll drag you all with me."

Before Emma could react, Ash produced a scalpel from her pocket and swiftly slashed it across Emma's leg. Emma recoiled in agony, feeling the blade tear through the fabric of her scrubs and leaving a deep cut across her calf.

"SHIT!" Emma's cry echoed through the rain-soaked air as she collapsed to the ground, clutching her leg in pain. Her eyes squeezed shut as she gritted her teeth against the searing sensation.

"You're pathetic." Ash muttered as she stood up. "So fucking pathetic. I can't believe you. I can't believe that you'd even *try* to disobey me like that. You're a heartless creature, a murderer, a monster."

"I'm the monster that you created."

"I know." Said Ash. "You were my proudest creation, but you betrayed me, and now I have to put you back in your place. *Now I have to show you how cold my heart really is.*"

With each step Ash took closer, Emma retreated in fear, realizing the vulnerability and danger of her situation. She could only hope that Ash wouldn't follow through with the arson she was planning. "Ash, please… It's not too late to change, I understand that you're scared, but—"

"You'd lose your fucking mind trying to understand me, Emma. You can't help me. Nothing will. You're a murderer like me. You don't deserve to live, and neither do I."

Ash had literally forced Emma to the brink, her body teetering on the floor mere inches from a four-story drop. In that precarious moment, the line between life and death blurred, the prospect of survival dwindling to near impossibility. With a deep wound searing her leg and fear gripping her soul, Emma found herself immobilized, drained of strength.

"Kill me," Emma cried aloud. "just promise that you'll turn yourself into the police. Please…"

"That was your job. Your chance to get me arrested has passed," Ash said with a look of despise in her eyes. "I'll see you in hell."

With sudden force, Ash placed her foot on Emma's head before kicking her off the roof. A few seconds later, she looked over the edge.

Emma lay dead, her blood splattered across the concrete floor, forming a growing puddle, reminiscent of a watermelon dropped from a great height. As it was the side of the hospital, nobody witnessed the fall, but it would be a gruesome sight for whoever discovered the body up close.

Ash stared with a blank expression. It was typical for her not to feel guilty or upset after murdering someone, but the usual excitement was absent. There was no sense of achievement, no excitement, no gain. Murdering Emma felt more like a chore than anything else, which Ash simply walked away from once it was done.

It was time for the main event.

Chapter 11
Burning sins

12:00 PM.

Anderson was leaning comfortably in his chair, legs crossed on his desk, with his head resting on his arms. The news of Kat's murderer being apprehended finally granted him a moment of peace. "Feels so good being able to relax for once." Anderson said with a sigh of relief. "Last night, I had the best sleep that I've had in years!"

"That's good." replied from the chair opposite his desk, her legs huddled into her stomach. Anderson had invited her to spend her lunch break with him in his office to 'keep him company', as he enjoyed Charlotte's presence. She reminded him of Kat. "I spent last night talking to Emma, then I relaxed with my boyfriend for the rest of the night."

There were four knocks on the door followed by David walking into the room. Anderson was pleased to see him, inviting him to sit down on the other empty chair.

"I've got some good news and some bad news." David announced.

"Start off with the good news, but I'm sure there's nothing too bad." Anderson replied.

"The good news is that the person the police arrested yesterday was in fact the person who murdered the oncology patient." David said before announcing the bad news. "The bad news is that there was a flaw in the interview."

Charlotte listened intently as David continued. Anderson had briefed her on the murders, particularly Kat's case.

"When the interviewer asked him about other murders, such as Quinn and Kat, the suspect was visually confused and was proven to have not killed the two."

Anderson's heart dropped. "Does that mean..."

"Yes." Said David. "There is still a murderer at the hospital. The police will be returning soon for further investigation."

David went on to discuss Daniel Graham's autopsy, revealing that he had been poisoned with cyanide. "Other staff have reported feeling sick with similar symptoms, fortunately, none have died. However, the murder is most likely linked to Justin Miller's death."

The conversation shifted to Justin's demise. Anderson revealed that he was accidentally killed by Emma due to a venous air embolism, a detail Charlotte was unaware of.

David suggested bringing Emma in for further investigation, but Anderson objected. He had witnessed Emma's reaction upon discovering Quinn's body and believed that was sufficient evidence to prove she wouldn't murder anyone else.

"That's not how the world works, Joel," said David. "Murders often act innocent, deceiving and tricking detectives. You can't ignore suspects because you think they would never commit such a crime, because the truth is, they would. The nicest person in the world is just as capable of committing horrific crimes as the world's greatest murderer."

"But why?" Anderson asked, able to comprehend why someone as seemingly innocent as Emma would commit such an act.

"Mental illness, manipulation, force, revenge – there are millions," said David. "Some do it for personal gain, others do it for nothing."

As Charlotte continued to listen, things started to add up. She thought about the walk she and Emma had taken the night before. *Mental health*. Emma admitted that she had been struggling with her mental health. *Manipulation*. She described Ash as an awful person who made her feel horrible. *Force*. Emma had mentioned that Ash forced her to do tasks she didn't want to do. *Revenge*. *What revenge would she want…?*

Suddenly, Charlotte remembered the sentence Emma had said the night before.

"*It does, especially after a life has been lost… She blames it on me. It makes me feel like… like…*"

Like a *murderer*. That's what she was saying.

Staring at the desk in disbelief, Charlotte muttered, "Emma…"

The two men's heads turned to look at Charlotte as she muttered. They noticed the horrified expression on her face, as if she had stumbled upon something she wasn't supposed to know.

"Nurse Ash… Do you know anything about her?" Charlotte asked desperately.

David shrugged while Anderson thought. "She recently lost her daughter, but that's all I know."

Charlotte had no idea that Ash was a mother. She was clueless.

'*Revenge. Ash used Emma for revenge*.'

Last night, Emma said, "*It feels like I'm being controlled by pressure and anxiety. If I do something wrong, if I'm pushed to the edge, I don't know if I'll be safe.*"

Charlotte finally realized what Emma meant. She wasn't putting herself in danger – Ash was putting her in danger. Ash is the pressure and anxiety. Ash is the reason she's been pushed over the edge; Ash is the reason that Emma isn't…

"Emma's not safe," Charlotte announced. "Something's wrong, I know it is, she needs help…"

"What? What do you mean?" David asked in confusion.

Charlotte quickly stood up in a rush. Her words burst out of her mouth as she tried to quickly tell the two men what had happened before it's too late. "Ash is the murderer. Nurse Ash. She's... I can't believe it, why didn't I notice sooner..."

Suddenly, the fire alarm began to scream across the hospital, taking the three by shock.

"Is this a drill? What's going on?" David panicked. Anderson stood still in shock. This wasn't a drill, there was a fire.

"It's Ash, God damn it! This isn't a drill, get out!" Charlotte exclaimed, running towards the door.

10 minutes earlier...

Emma's betrayal of Ash wasn't part of her plan, but to save Evelyn, she had to make compromises. Initially, Ash planned for Emma to sneak Evelyn out of the hospital while Ash initiated the fire. However, circumstances forced her to change course. Now, she had to start the fire herself before rescuing Evelyn.

Ash made her way to the staircase, traversing from the roof to the basement. Unfamiliar with the layout, she quickly located the hospital's electrical distribution room. After stealthily entering, she ensured the room was empty, finding herself alone amidst a vast expanse of grey walls adorned with large metal switchbox cabinets. Each cabinet bore labels such as "OPERATING ROOM 1", another saying "DEPARTMENT 4B," with countless wires and pipes adorning the walls, the only sound being the hum of electricity.

Locating the cabinet "STORAGE UNIT A1," the hospital's primary storage room, Ash knew it was stocked with flammable materials like paper, medication, bed sheets, gowns, and oxygen tanks. After cutting off the electrical supply to the room, a risky move with the potential for discovery by maintenance workers, Ash proceeded to create short circuits by manipulating the wires. With her stolen scalpel, she stripped the wires of their insulation, inserting her beloved notebook between them, a relic of her dark intentions now serving a pivotal role.

Lighting a cigarette with her lighter, Ash took a deep drag before placing it among the exposed wires. With nerves and excitement intertwining, she prepared to restore power to the room and flee. Anticipation coursed through her veins as she envisioned the chain reaction: the faulty wiring igniting the flammable materials, engulfing the storage room in flames within moments. The inferno would spread, consuming adjacent areas and potentially engulfing the entire hospital in chaos.

In the electrical room, Ash's notebook and lighter would trigger an explosion in the storage room cabinet, initiating a domino effect that would engulf the surrounding cabinets in flames.

"The lack of security in this damn shithole is the reason for its own downfall." Ash muttered, taking another drag from her cigarette. With no time to spare, she discarded the cigarette and activated the power to the storage room.

The countdown began. Ash raced out of the room and sprinted up the staircase to the second floor where Evelyn awaited.

Upon reaching the second floor, the piercing wail of the fire alarm greeted Ash.

'Shit, already? How fast did that fire spread?!' she exclaimed to herself, pushing aside her questions. Her priority was to locate Evelyn and evacuate swiftly.

Bursting into the children's ward, Ash's frantic search yielded no sign of Evelyn. Panic gripped her as she realized the bed was empty, immaculately made, suggesting Evelyn had been discharged.

'*But she was still sick, she can't have been discharged...*' Ash thought, cursing her oversight regarding Evelyn's surgery.

Ash then remembered about the surgery. '*Shit, it was today?!*'

She could only stand and laugh at her stupid mistake. She didn't find it funny, she found it absolutely idiotic. It made her furious.

'*Why didn't I fucking check when it was?*'

With time slipping away, Ash faced the grim reality of the situation. Patients typically evacuated during fires, but the magnitude of this blaze threatened the entire hospital. "I have to find Evelyn… or she's going to be like Ellie," Ash resolved, her determination reignited.

With a newfound motivation, Ash dashed towards the pre-op area. The hospital, now resembling an apocalypse, lay eerily deserted, frozen in chaos.

As Ash raced down the corridor, the acrid scent of smoke permeated the air. Turning a corner towards the pre-operation ward, she was met with a daunting sight—a raging inferno consuming the 'General Surgery' wing.

"*Please… Please keep Evelyn safe.*" Ash pleaded desperately, her heart heavy with fear. "*Please, please, please…*"

With the fire advancing rapidly, she turned her focus to survival. Other wards ignited in succession, signalling the dire extent of the blaze. With the first floor engulfed, Ash's only recourse was to ascend to higher ground or locate an emergency exit amidst the chaos.

12:20 PM

Charlotte raced through the hospital corridors, her frantic search for Emma or Ash, just someone to confirm that Emma was safe. But she was nowhere to be seen. The acrid stench of smoke hung heavy in the air, exacerbating her difficulty in breathing, especially given her asthma.

Having scoured the children's department to no luck, Charlotte realized the danger of her situation amidst the spreading inferno. With a sense of urgency, she dashed back towards the first floor in a bid to escape the engulfing flames. However, her path was obstructed by the relentless advance of the fire, with the emergency department and surgery wing ablaze.

Desperation clawed at her as she surveyed her dwindling options, her eyes falling upon another problem.

'Is that... Ash...?'

It was indeed Ash. She stared blankly at the blonde.

"You did this, you evil bitch!" Charlotte's accusation rang out over the blaring alarms as she confronted Ash.

Approaching Charlotte with an unsettling calmness, Ash acknowledged her role in the chaos. "I did. Well done for figuring it out. How did you know?" she inquired, unfazed by Charlotte's outrage.

"This is not the time for conversation, you idiot! We need to get out of here!" Charlotte retorted, attempting to push past Ash, only to be halted in her tracks.

"You're not escaping." Ash declared ominously. "You're going to burn."

"What?! Are you mad?!"

"I am. I'm furious. I'm insane, I'm a monster, I'm your enemy, I'm everyone's enemy," Ash spat, her words dripping with bitterness. "I'm dragging you and everyone else to hell with me."

"Burn here all you want, you deserve it, but I'm going!" Charlotte declared, attempting to shove Ash aside, only to be met with a firm grip on her arm.

"I said you're going to burn with me, or you're going to burn alone. Choose now."

Charlotte found herself paralyzed, the smoke choking her lungs, rendering her unable to respond.

"Burn alone then." Ash sneered, forcibly ushering Charlotte into the nearby janitor's closet – the very same closet where Kat met her demise.

As Charlotte collapsed to the ground, her asthma rendered her helpless, gasping for precious breaths amidst the stifling smoke. Though spared from immediate flames, the tightening grip of her condition left her vulnerable and incapacitated.

Luckily the room wasn't on fire, in fact it probably had fresher air than the corridor, but the effects of Charlotte's asthma had already begun to take place. Her chest felt tight and wheezy, but no matter how much she tried to inhale, she couldn't possibly grab hold of the oxygen she desperately needed.

"Now, play dead." Ash commanded coldly before departing, leaving Charlotte alone in the suffocating darkness of the closet, her fate hanging in the balance amidst the chaos of the inferno.

12:25 PM

April was searching through the crowds of patients, staff and visitors, who were all standing in the hospital carpark, staring at a tragedy unfold before their eyes. Charlotte couldn't be found anywhere, neither could Ash or Emma.

When she spotted Anderson, she decided to approach him to ask if he knew where Charlotte was. Charlotte had recently told her that they were getting along pretty well, so he might know.

"Mister Anderson, have you seen Charlotte? I'm April, one of her friends."

Anderson looked at her with concern. "She's in there looking for Emma."

"What?!" April exclaimed. "She has asthma, is she crazy?!"

As April rushed past, David said. "Don't, you're putting your own life in danger."

"Charlotte has done more for me than I could ever ask for, I'm going to save her."

As April ran towards the hospital, David said, "Those kids are insane, going into a burning building?!"

The front entrance engulfed in flames, April made her way into the building through an emergency exit. Racing down the smoky corridors, she called out Charlotte's name, but her voice was drowned out by the blaring alarms.

With each breath, the smoke tightened around her lungs, inducing a growing sense of panic. Though the smoke wasn't thick, it was enough to stir regret for her choices. Nevertheless, already inside the burning hospital, she decided not to leave without Charlotte by her side.

As she passed each room, she peered through the windows, searching for signs of life. Every room appeared either deserted or inaccessible, but as she approached the right side of the hospital, she encountered more and more rooms consumed by fire until she had nowhere else to turn.

Witnessing the fire firsthand sent shivers down her spine. The intense, bright orange glow radiated heat and danger, a menacing force beyond her control. Despite the urgency, there was one room in the hallway she hadn't yet investigated. Initially tempted to overlook it due to its small size, she hesitated.

Thankfully, she chose to check. As she approached, she noticed the window obscured by a thin layer of dark grey smoke. With a quick swipe, she revealed a chilling sight—a motionless figure within.

It was Charlotte, and she wasn't moving.

"Charlotte!" April shouted through the window.

She heard it. Charlotte shifted her head slightly, trying to locate the source of the call, but the darkened window obscured her view.

"Stay with me, Charlotte, I'll get you out of there!" April yelled, attempting to open the door, only to find it locked. She needed to find another way in.

"Damn it, I need to think fast..." April muttered to herself, her eyes darting nervously as the fire crept closer. The sight of the smoke patching up and darkening indicated the increasing danger.

Suddenly, the power went out, plunging the surroundings into darkness, save for the flickering light from the fire down the hallway. April retrieved her phone from her pocket and activated the flashlight to illuminate her surroundings. Just beyond the janitor's closet lay the pharmacy, its chairs clustered next to the desks. With urgency, April dashed to the pharmacy, her hands grasping one of the black wheelie chairs, their surfaces coated in soot, which transferred onto Charlotte's hands as April pulled her to safety.

Returning to the storage room with the wheelie chair, April yelled through the window, "Move, I'm smashing the window open!"

Charlotte barely reacted; her immobility painfully evident. Time was running out, though. The flames had reached the doors leading to the emergency department, indicating the fire would soon engulf the hallway.

With a surge of determination, April struck the chair against the window. Despite her efforts, the impact caused only minor damage, leaving a few cracks.

Undeterred, she struck again, and again, but the stubborn window refused to shatter.

As the fire encroached upon the pharmacy, the air filled with pitch-black smoke. The urgency now left the two women with mere seconds to flee.

With a final strike, the window shattered. Some of the glass inflicted cuts on Charlotte, but wounds could be tended to; the threat of death loomed far more menacingly.

"C'mon," April coughed, her voice strained. "Over here, Charlotte, please…"

Despite relentless coughing, Charlotte summoned the last remnants of her strength. She dragged herself across the floor, the broken glass cutting into her palms, eliciting groans of pain.

Summoning every ounce of energy, April seized Charlotte's hand and pulled her out of the window, their escape now a desperate race against time.

"Come on, hold onto me. We're getting out of here alive," April urged, guiding Charlotte's arm around her shoulder. The blonde struggled to walk, her strength waning with each step, while April felt her own energy draining rapidly.

'I'm going to escape... with charlotte... no matter what.' April silently vowed.

The sight of the emergency exit's light beckoned like a beacon of hope. It was their lifeline, their salvation. Summoning every ounce of remaining strength, April propelled herself forward, dragging Charlotte along in a desperate sprint.

At the exit, a team of firefighters and paramedics from another hospital awaited them. As soon as Charlotte and April emerged into the open air, they gasped for breath, their lungs grateful for the respite.

Ash was trapped. After locking Charlotte in the janitor's closet, she hurried to the main entrance in attempt to leave the building, only to discover it blocked by flames. The rooms beside her were sealed shut, and the emergency exit, her only alternative, was also engulfed in fire.

Ash gazed helplessly at the mesmerising flames before her. They danced with an insatiable hunger, devouring everything in their path. Despite the devastation unfolding, a faint smile graced her lips as she watched all her troubles burning away before her. Though uncertain of Evelyn's fate, she found solace in the hope that someone within the hospital had come to her rescue.

As the smoke thickened, Ash felt her legs buckle beneath her, weakened by the toxic fumes. Collapsing to the ground, she gasped for air, her lungs burning with each breath. In the chaos, her silver cross necklace shattered upon impact, its fragments scattering across the hallway. Summoning her remaining strength, Ash crawled on all fours, her hands reaching out to retrieve the broken pendant before tenderly pressing it against her chest.

"It's beautiful… My masterpiece, my final act of liberation, purging this place of its sins," she muttered, her voice carrying an eerie determination. "They all deserve this fate, every single one of them… The doctors with their god complexes, the nurses with their face smiles, the patients trapped in their own misery. They're all part of my game, players in a twisted symphony orchestrated by fate."

Her words grew more fervent, fuelled by a madness bordering on obsession. "Flames, burn my skin. Let me suffer… Don't let God ease my pain. Light my darkness with your fire. Fill my lungs with black smoke. Let the heat of my sins burn my skin and scorch my soul."

With a final act of resignation, she collapsed onto the floor, curling into a tight circle. Clutching the cross to her heart, she whispered, "My sweet baby girl is dancing amidst the fireflies. Her laughter echoing in the crackle of flames. She's there, just beyond the reach of my fingertips, beckoning me to join her in that eternal embrace. My angel is guiding me home. Now, take my life, you monstrous flame… Let me rest with my daughter. Put an end to this nightmare."

Chapter 12
The Maple Murders.

The Maple News – January 18th 2023

Tragic Blaze at Maple Hospital: Arsonist Convicted of Murder, Lives Lost in Devastating Inferno

In a harrowing turn of events, Maple Hospital, once a beacon of healing within our community, has been reduced to ashes following a deadly arson attack perpetrated by a 44-year-old woman. Identified as Ash Thomas, the perpetrator was swiftly apprehended on January 17th, 2023, after authorities discovered her culpability in not only igniting a blaze that engulfed the hospital but also in the cold-blooded murder of five individuals within its walls.

Following a thorough investigation by law enforcement agencies, Ash was brought to trial, where she was found guilty of her heinous crimes. In a courtroom packed with sorrowful spectators, the presiding judge delivered the solemn verdict, sentencing the convicted murderer to life imprisonment without the possibility of parole.

"The loss of lives and the destruction of Maple Hospital is a tragedy that will forever haunt our community," remarked Joel Anderson, the hospital director, his voice heavy with grief. "Our hearts ache for the families who have been torn apart by this senseless act of violence. Yet, even in the face of such devastation, we must find solace in the resilience of our community and the unwavering dedication of our healthcare professionals to continue serving those in need."

The tragedy at Maple Hospital, however, extends far beyond the confines of the courtroom. The inferno, sparked by Ash's callous actions, claimed the lives of twenty-one individuals, with an additional thirty-three sustaining injuries in the chaotic evacuation that ensued. Amidst the chaos, over three hundred staff members, patients, and visitors were forced to flee for their lives, their sense of security shattered by the flames that consumed the once-thriving medical facility.

As our community grapples with the profound loss and devastation wrought by this senseless act of violence, we extend our deepest sympathies to the families and loved ones of those who perished in the fire. Maple Hospital may have fallen, but the resilience and compassion of our community will endure as we come together to support one another in the wake of this tragedy.

One year and four months later…

April 9th, 2024, 9:00 AM.

Under the early spring sunlight, freshly bloomed daffodils swayed gracefully in the soft breeze, their golden hues radiating warmth. The light blue skies added to the cheerful ambiance. Following just over a year of reconstruction, fundraising efforts, and support from charities and benefactors, Maple Hospital stood proudly rebuilt.

The new hospital boasted a modern, slightly expanded design, maintaining its vibrant and welcoming aesthetic. Charlotte and April, along with both new and familiar faces among the staff, gathered opposite the entrance. Nearby, reporters and photographers eagerly awaited to document the reopening of the hospital, marking a significant milestone after its tragic past.

An orange ribbon adorned the entrance, signalling the commencement of the ceremony. Standing poised with a pair of oversized scissors was the new hospital director, Mrs. Rebecca Howells, ready to officially inaugurate the facility. The retirement of Anderson, who had faced discrimination following the fire, marked a transition as Mrs. Howells assumed leadership.

Charlotte peered through the glass doors from afar, a mix of excitement and nervousness churning in her stomach. While memories of the old hospital lingered, she reminded herself that this was a fresh start — a new beginning.

'Emma would've been so excited to see this.' wistful smile. Her thoughts were interrupted by a buzz from her pocket. Retrieving her phone, Charlotte discovered a message from her boyfriend, Ryan: a video of Evelyn.

"Say good luck to mommy with her first day back at work!" Ryan's voice echoed from the video as Evelyn chirped, "Good luck mom with your first day back at work!"

Charlotte's heart swelled with warmth as she watched the video. A few weeks after the fire, Evelyn had been taken from her foster parents, prompting Charlotte and Ryan to step in as her foster parents. Despite the challenges, they had embraced Evelyn with boundless love. In February, they made it official and adopted her—a significant milestone for the young couple and a testament to their commitment to their newfound family.

David continued his work at the hospital, serving as the chief pathologist. While some staff returned to their positions, others departed, making room for new members to join the team. Meanwhile, Ash's fate took a definitive turn when firefighters rescued her from the blaze, finding her unconscious. After a day in the hospital, she was sentenced to life in prison for a total of 26 murders.

"Thank goodness the chaos has ended." April remarked, standing beside Charlotte.

"Yeah, it's a relief," Charlotte concurred, her voice tinged with solemnity. "The end of a tragedy. The end of the Maple Murders."

April placed a reassuring hand on Charlotte's shoulder. "Ready to begin your shift, nurse Charlotte?" she asked, her smile warm and encouraging as the spring's sun.

Charlotte returned the smile, her grin widening at the sound of her new title. *'Nurse Charlotte,'* she repeated to herself, still getting used to the change. Having transitioned from a medical student to a registered nurse after graduating from university, the moment felt surreal yet exhilarating.

"Absolutely," Charlotte replied confidently. "What about you, nurse April?"

"Ready."

The crowd cheered as Mrs Howells cut the ribbon. Hand in hand, Charlotte and April, along with everybody else, entered the hospital.

And so, spring turned to summer, summer turned to autumn and autumn turned to winter. April started a relationship with another doctor, soon after Charlotte and Ryan got married, and they all continued to work diligently at the hospital, serving their community with dedication and compassion.

The memories of the tragic events that had unfolded in the past were not forgotten, but they served as a reminder of the resilience and strength of the human spirit.

As the years passed, the rebuilt hospital flourished, becoming a beacon of hope and healing in the town. Charlotte and April remained close friends, supporting each other through the highs and lows of life. And as for Evelyn, she thrived under the loving care of Charlotte and Ryan, growing into a bright and spirited young girl who brought joy to everyone around her.

Through it all, the shadow of the Maple Murders faded into the past, replaced by the bright promise of a future filled with hope, love, and new beginnings. And as Charlotte looked back on the journey that had brought her to this moment, she knew that while the scars of the past would always remain, they would never define her future. With a sense of gratitude and determination, she embraced the endless possibilities that lay ahead, ready to face whatever challenges may come with unwavering resolve.

And so, as the sun set on another day at Maple Hospital, Charlotte smiled, knowing that she was exactly where she was meant to be.

The end.

Author's note

Thank you so much for reading my novel. It's only short, but I'm so glad I could make my idea from 2022 come to life. I apologize for anything that isn't completely correct or realistic, finding research on how to commit arson isn't easy haha, but hey, it's a fictional world based on a Roblox game, it doesn't matter if the odd thing is wrong.

I would like to thank my 48,000 followers on Tik Tok for supporting me with this idea and my wonderful friends and family who inspired me to create the characters and story.

Printed in Great Britain
by Amazon